"Want is for those who seek comfort,
we seek peace. Find the missing halves and all will
turn in your favor, but be warned, the darkness and the
light hold a secret no one can understand."

Rebellion: A Seven Generals Novel
Book One
© 2022 S. G. Blinn
Editor: Sarah Hawkins

ISBN: 979-8-9862372-0-6

Printed in the United States of America

Content Warning: **Domestic Violence**

Visit my website at www.sgblinn.com

Rebellion

A SEVEN GENERALS
NOVEL

BOOK ONE

BY S. G. BLINN

This book is dedicated to those who strive for freedom. Never allow yourself to be forgotten; use your voice and strength will follow.

I

It was an endless nightmare. Screams filled the shadows, and the light, splattered with carnage. No one could remember when the fighting had begun, but they quickly realized that no one was safe. It did not matter if you were mortal or immortal, Hellion or Heaven-sent, everyone was a target. Which meant anyone could be the enemy.

"What do we have?" the doctor yelled.

"One unidentified female. No age or status of birth known," the nurse replied.

Drip. Drop. The tiles in every Human hospital were always white and pristine. It collected the blood droplets from the violence outside its doors, a chaos that seemed never-ending for those trying to save a life.

"Where did she come from?" the doctor asked.

The nurse rushed forward, keeping up with the gurney. "Dr. Eddison by personal vehicle. He instructed the medical team on how to handle her once he got here."

This was the emergency room of a busy hospital. They had no time to ask questions—those came later—but when the light shined on her lifeless body, they all were taken aback by what they discovered.

Her face was torn with visible bone and muscle. While hands slowly peeled away the debris and blankets, a large hole was discovered in the center of her chest. Her ribs were broken and jagged, creating a sharp obstacle they had to avoid.

"This is horrible . . ."

This small, lifeless woman was torn apart. The armies of Heaven and Hell were ruthless to anyone they touched. Her blood was mixed with the dirt from the attack site, and vitals were almost impossible to record. They needed to find a heartbeat, a sign of life, to determine if this woman could be saved.

"The Hellion attack had left nothing but ash and heartbreak. With the Heaven-sent retaliating, all those stuck in the middle are left looking for a miracle. Will their lives be spared from those who descended from the sky or crawled their way from the pits . . .?"

The news spoke of the destruction. How Angels, Demons, magic, and immortals were fighting. It was all for power, control, and a need to dominate. A need slowly tearing this world apart.

A slight beep on a machine caused the nurses surrounding the woman to react. "She is alive!"

It was a hopeful moment, one instantly shattered when more of the woman's skin was revealed. Small markings littered her body, familiar symbols that caused all movement to cease. Every Human trying to save her took a large step back.

"The markings on her body indicate she is a sacrifice to the gods!" the doctor yelled. "Get me Dr. Eddison!"

Sacrifice. That woman was chained to a wooden beam with markings burned into her skin. Those poles were everywhere. It was an offering to those who served their master. To be labeled a sacrifice was a death sentence, and all knew never to disturb such a feast. A piece of knowledge that Dr. Eddison chose to ignore which was out of character for him.

"Dr. Eddison!"

The nurse spared no time in finding the man responsible for bringing the sacrifice to their doorstep. She was a beacon for the Demons who would devour her body and soul. This woman needed to leave no matter how injured she was; her being there was a risk to everyone at the hospital.

"I may not work in the emergency room, but there was a reason I requested to take control of the patient."

He acted like he didn't know the rules. Humans were nothing more than collateral damage in a war they truly did not understand. To choose a side meant survival and protection, but Dr. Eddison refused.

"The—"

Eddison did not give her a chance to speak. "Call the chief of medicine, I already have been granted the ability to treat the individual in question, and once she is stable, she will be moved."

She didn't know what else to say. Eddison walked away from her and towards the large group that had gathered. There was no way he could turn away from her the moment he saw the horrors she'd faced. He was drawn to her in a way he could not put into words.

11

"Dr. Eddison," the emergency room doctor said but Eddison ignored him.

This hospital was in a territory controlled by Hell. Demons and their soldiers were not an uncommon sight, but the only reason Dr. Eddison was allowed to work here was his experience. He was the only individual with a unique knowledge of creatures from Heaven and Hell. No one knew how he knew so much, but he was trusted, at least for now.

"The chief has confirmed Dr. Eddison's claims," the nurse explained to the group.

There was no shock on Eddison's face. This was like any other patient, one that needed to be treated with care. With ease, he inserted an IV into her arm and began his assessment. Creatures from Hell had blood that reflected their darkened souls and Heaven had blood as yellow as the sun, but this woman had blood of gold. It was an observation he noted along with her other injuries.

Eddison leaned in. "I know you can hear me. My name is Dr. Eddison, and I will be piecing your body back together. You are safe. I claim no loyalty to Heaven nor Hell; you are in no danger from me."

He felt the need to introduce himself, even if she was unconscious. The knowledge about the anatomy of Hellion creatures varied due to their diversity. What the other doctors saw as a faint single heartbeat didn't mean she was dead or dying. His chart continued to grow as his observation continued.

The chest wound. The internal organs were already starting to repair themselves but needed a clean line to heal properly. Snap. Crack. Eddison broke each exposed rib by hand and carefully set them back into place. Next, her skin.

It was gone, with decaying muscle exposed. What little he could find had the marks of the sacrifice. He put clotting foam in the exposed areas—even though she wasn't Human, the risk of infection was still a problem.

"What did they do to you . . .," he muttered.

Claw and teeth marks were everywhere. With each mark documented, he turned his attention to the wire bound to her back. To remove it would cause the body more trauma, but while removing the blanket, a black feather fell to the floor.

Peeling it away, more feathers were discovered, and wings exposed. They were darker than a moonless sky, broken and ripped apart. These types of feathers were not on Demonic or Hellion creatures, they were reserved for Angelic beings. Never had he read or witnessed Angels with dark wings and served as a sacrifice. A need to touch them became too great to ignore.

Eddison reached out and the soft tip turned sharp upon contact. It cut through his glove and red blood slowly dripped from his hand. Each pull and movement to the body caused no reaction. The gentle hum from the machines around her still showed no signs of life.

"Almost done . . ."

Eddison kept talking to her, gentle whispers letting her know what was happening. His name tag hung from his belt, and it only had a single name: Eddison, with his credentials following the name.

*

Everyone walked past the quarantined room; no one went in without Dr. Eddison's permission. His office was the only one that held books because he didn't trust technology. The puzzle of who this woman could be had stumped him.

"Dr. Eddison?" a voice called out from the other side of his office door.

Golden blood. Black wings. She had Human qualities. No scales, horns, tails, or any indication of a Hellion birth. Those black wings were of Angelic properties but didn't have the color characteristics. These pieces didn't fit, and it frustrated him.

"Dr. Eddison, may I have a word?"

The knock is what took him out of his musings. Dr. Eddison's violet eyes showed his blood was linked to a Wiccan clan. Magic coursed through his veins, which gave him the religious exemption from Human society. Those eyes created a target, but he didn't fear death. If it was his time, he would be ready.

Without knocking a second time, the chief of medicine walked into the office and frowned. He saw all the books and educational materials sprawled over every surface. Eddison hadn't slept, not since she came to the hospital, which put everyone on edge.

"You here to lecture me too?" Eddison called out, finally meeting his boss's gaze.

"No," the man began. "You know what you did, but that woman cannot stay here."

14

"I know" was Eddison's only reply.

"I do not think you do. Forgive me, Dr. Eddison, but we do not know why she was sacrificed. Something could come after her."

The older man didn't approach the doctor, but he tried to use his words to express his worry. Humans were at a disadvantage in this war and had to protect themselves any way they saw fit. By him expressing his concerns, he meant Eddison didn't have the resources of this hospital much longer.

"She was found alive after the Hellions had their fill. How she survived I have yet to discover, but the marks are nothing more than scars. They cannot track her."

Eddison's explanation was supposed to comfort the Human in front of him, but it only caused the man to worry harder.

"We cannot thank you enough for all you have done for us, Dr. Eddison—"

"I can't stay," he interjected.

"But—"

Eddison slowly stood. "I will monitor the sacrifice, and when she is ready to be moved, I will see she leaves the hospital as requested."

"She isn't Human," the chief muttered.

He wasn't a man to judge based on race, but Eddison was nervous. The lights above their heads flickered. Fights had always been waged without any indication of remorse for the Humans caught in the middle. Hospitals were never targeted but had been destroyed. With the ground slowly shaking beneath their feet, movement was heard outside the door.

"The news said the battles were over fifty miles away."

Eddison's eyes traveled to the ceiling. Without a moment to blink, the window in the room cracked and a pressure forced both men to the ground. A high-pitched screech filled their ears, causing them to hold their heads tightly.

Creak. A large, lengthy creature crawled its way into the office through the broken window. Its body was made of bones and decaying flesh. Sharp teeth were observed when it looked around the room.

It had no eyes, but when it focused in Eddison's direction, the creature growled. Black vines formed from the creature's feet and wrapped around both men. Trapped, they both watched it slowly get closer and closer. When it reached for Eddison, something appeared between them, causing the creature to scream.

Cold droplets fell over Eddison's leg as she stood there holding the creature's outstretched arm. Her body was bandaged from the care Eddison showed, with her wings wrapped tightly to her body. As the creature moved, a stain on her hospital gown slowly started to grow with golden blood.

"Eddison!" the chief yelled.

He couldn't look away. A strong gust caused her hair to move violently around her. Blood pooled from the bandage that covered her eyes, but she could sense where this creature was with ease.

A simple movement took the arm off the creature. She threw it across the room. It screeched, filling the room with the rage and pain it now experienced. The woman went to yell but nothing came out. A faded scar existed around her lips from a bind. Those barbaric contraptions took away a person's ability to speak, creating total submission from those under their control.

The agony on her face broke his heart. She was in pain, but her weightless body slowly backed up till she was standing on his chest. She was small, only five foot three. When the creature charged, he reached out and took hold of her legs.

The touch startled the woman. She kicked him hard before jumping forward to meet the creature. It happened fast. The woman moved through it, her body ripping it apart from the inside. She was covered in the residue when the woman reemerged. She killed it; and when the vines disappeared, Eddison rushed forward to catch her before she fell to the ground.

*

"The most recent attacks left most of the city in distress. Numerous buildings have been destroyed with hundreds of residents currently on their way to this hospital," the chief began.

"Do we know what happened?"

"Why are they doing this?"

"Should we be evacuating?"

17

The chief of medicine raised his hands to silence the questions from all the concerned hospital staff in front of him. "This is nothing we haven't seen before; everyone will need to work together—"

"Is Dr. Eddison still here? Will he be able to help us?"

The chief frowned. "Dr. Eddison is only one man. He is currently preoccupied, but our safety cannot be put in his hands. It is a gift to have him here to educate us, but we cannot rely on him to do what needs to be done."

He was right. Fear made people panic, which caused them to retreat. This hospital was run by Humans, but with the affiliations and protection of Hell, creatures found their way through their doors. Why that creature attacked this building left everyone flabbergasted, but Eddison: he stood in that woman's room, motionless.

"I will not hurt you," he whispered.

The woman stood behind him, holding a scalpel to his throat. To heal so quickly from such a massive trauma showed her strength, and how she easily pinned him against the wall showed her courage. Eddison was over a foot taller than her, yet she held him up by his neck. He still couldn't see her eyes, but he could tell she was upset.

"I know you are scared, but you are safe."

Those words caused her to squeeze harder. A howl in the hallway echoed in the distance, but she was focused solely on Eddison. Even when she dropped him on the ground, she never looked away. She was waiting for something on the other side of the door. It wanted to get in.

"Run!" Screams filled the hallway outside the room.

18

The door was forced open as a doglike beast walked in. It focused on her, waiting for permission to act.

"You—"

The woman looked towards the beast before coughing hard. Eddison's train of thought ceased when she looked down to the blood on her hand. She continued to cough, but that beast refused to let Eddison get close.

"If you are a Hellion, you are safe," he said calmly, taking a step forward.

"But by how you are running, you have Heavenly blood in your veins—"

The creature growled when he got too close. The woman's body was weak. She started to shake but refused to show any weakness. Slowly, she lost her footing, and the creature was there to catch her fall. It was impossible to heal from all her wounds in such a short period of time. No matter the power, a body needed to heal.

"I am not going to hurt her."

Eddison didn't know if the creature could understand him. By the shape of its body and its mannerisms, he knew it was a hellhound. They solely exist to serve their master. If this woman was its master, it would protect her, but it also wouldn't attack unless ordered.

"She cannot stay here."

Each step he took was slow. He made sure the creature could see him, and thankfully, it didn't attack when he lifted her frail body once more. A need consumed him. A want to claim and protect this woman overtook his ability to be logical, and rather than take her to a sanctuary, he took her home.

II

She had yet to wake up. Two weeks had passed, and her body battled itself to heal properly. It was on fire, even though her skin was ice. The woman now lay in his bed. No creatures found her here. She was safe.

Eddison didn't have a television. Books littered the living space, and notes of the golden-blooded Hellion was all he focused on. Never did any of his encounters or teachings indicate the significance of golden blood.

"Hello . . ."

Black wings. Only Angels had feathered wings with this build, but never had they been anything other than white. If the Angels fell, they would lose them entirely. Nowhere did it say anything about them turning black.

"Am I talking to myself?"

People would assume she was a Hellion, but she had the body of a Human. The barbaric practice of sacrifice was only reserved for Hellions, but the hellhounds that hid in the shadows of the apartment were drawn to their own kind. She was a Hellion with Angelic wings.

"You're distracted . . ."

Every time Eddison checked on the woman, the hounds let him pass. Not once did they attack but they never left the space. Eddison knew they sensed his blood. That scent would get him killed on either side, but for some reason, they left him alone.

"Eddison!" the voice said loud enough for him to realize someone else was in the apartment.

A man stood in his kitchen, arms crossed with an amused expression. "You're not dead?"

Wings of white were the first thing anyone saw of this man. His body showed he was a warrior, but his clothing was an ill attempt of blending into a place he didn't belong. But by Eddison not reacting to seeing the Angel in his home, he showed this wasn't the first time he entered without permission.

"Not yet," he replied.

Both sides might want Eddison dead, but he survived by making deals. Working with the Humans granted him sanctuary in their cities. They had enough doctors for Humans, but not enough for all the other species that existed in this world today.

"Damn," the Angel began.

"I thought I could finally get rid of you."

Malcom was his name, and he was Eddison's guardian Angel. The whole premise of guardianship was vague, and it took Eddison a long time to trust the Angel. But both men had a job to do and if the other played nice, no one was hurt.

"What do you want, Malcom?" Eddison asked.

His attention went from his house guest back to the notes sprawled all over the floor in front of him. Eddison needed answers. Malcom looked to the scattered papers and didn't pay attention to what was written. When he got to the drawing of the black wings, that playful attitude disappeared.

"Where did you see them?" the Angel asked, picking up the paper.

His voice was no louder than a whisper. Eddison could almost hear what he thought was fear. This Angel was a pain in his ass but didn't fear anything. That was what made guardians a fabled creature. They protected their charge, but why would an Angel want a Witch? Eddison gave up asking.

Malcom's reaction to his drawing confused him.

"Malcom—"

The Angel moved fast, appearing before Eddison and grabbing his shirt. Those bright eyes made sure Eddison was paying attention before he spoke. "This isn't a game."

"What are you talking about?"

Malcom's grip tightened. "Only a unique set of individuals have wings such as these. If you saw them without their army, it means this city is about to fall."

"You're talking non—"

Malcom refused to allow Eddison to speak; he needed the Witch to understand. "Where did you see them?"

"Let me go!" Eddison replied, matching the yell that came from the Angel's mouth.

Something moved in the shadows around them, but Malcom was too focused on Eddison to pay attention. "I smell death . . .," the Angel muttered.

A hound jumped from the shadows and knocked both men over. Before Malcom could register what happened, another hound appeared and bit his arm. The man grunted in pain, but Eddison was surprised the hounds were acting this way. The creatures had been inactive for weeks, leaving him alone.

Arms appeared behind Eddison and helped him stand. He didn't understand what was happening as those arms wrapped around him from behind. His eyes traveled to the black wings that wrapped around him and seemed to point at Malcom.

"Eddison!" Malcom struggled to yell.

Her eyes were like rubies. Red, rich rubies, and every time she blinked, they would sparkle. Eddison was mesmerized, ignoring the Angel's warning. Her face was gentle and flawless, but the power that leaked from her body made Malcom struggle to break free.

"Let him go!" the Angel yelled, but more hellhounds bit down into his flesh.

Her hands started to move with her fingers, forming patterns. Malcom didn't understand what she was doing, but Eddison remembered the mouthpiece he removed, the one that went all the way to her vocal cords. Since she couldn't speak, she must communicate through sign language.

"I will only give you one warning, Guardian, to leave my territory and not enter it again," Eddison translated, but when Malcom went to speak, the darkness seeped from her.

"Let him go!"

Her hands moved again: "This Witch is mine."

Eddison did not back away, did not move when she turned her body and brought her lips to his. The kiss was surprising, but his body reacted in a way he did not expect. It lit up like it was on fire. When she opened the kiss, he showed her how he was feeling.

Electrical shocks went to every part of his body. His hands reached up and touched her smooth skin, trying to bring her closer. He needed her closer, and rather than think logically, he let his body take over.

"No! Eddison, fight her! It is a trick!" Malcom screamed.

Eddison slowly broke the kiss but couldn't speak. He knew this wasn't logical, but he pulled her closer to him, making her body flush against his.

Malcom and the other Heaven-sent chose to keep the Humans in the dark regarding the Hellions they were fighting.

Eddison felt something deep inside that he didn't understand. If this was a trick, he was a fool to give in, but he lowered his mouth to hers once more, missing the action her wings created. The soft feathers became sharp as glass and sliced Malcom's throat. It took only a few moments for the Angel to lose his ability to speak and for her hounds to drag him away. She wanted her privacy.

Her wounds healed, even the scars from the wires he peeled from her skin had started to fade. His hands, they wanted to feel her, and when he realized she had changed into one of his shirts, he ripped the fabric from her body.

She did not stop him.

All she did was smirk. Her fingers gently combed through his bright red hair. Eddison couldn't speak, he was consumed by her. He didn't notice her nails elongate and find their way into his skull.

A wave of nausea hit him hard, causing his body to convulse. He turned away from her and threw up. The woman slowly peeled Eddison off her as he vomited. She didn't care if she was exposed; her eyes wandered to all the papers scattered around the apartment. Her eyes fell to the drawing of her wings.

She frowned. With a flick of her wrist, a green fire formed on the drawing of the wings, one that slowly consumed everything it touched. A hellfire. One that would always burn until everything it touched was destroyed. She wanted no evidence, but when her eyes traveled to the unconscious Wiccan doctor on the floor, a need to take him with her overpowered her judgement.

III

"In other news, a fire broke out in the Newton Town apartments. Multiple casualties were reported. The cause of the mysterious green flames is unknown."

Eddison heard a voice in the distance, one that got louder. His body hurt, a pain he never felt before. A pounding pressure in his head and a heaviness in his joints caused his waking to feel unnatural.

It took only a few moments before he realized that he was naked. When he tried to move something restricted his arms and legs. His lack of mobility didn't cause panic because his body and mind felt safe.

A hand reached over and forced him to lay down. The sound of the news broadcast faded, and all his attention went to her. The woman with red eyes covered his body with a dark velvet blanket.

"Where—" Eddison couldn't form a thought.

A basic instinct overtook his body when he noticed she was wearing a low-cut dress.

"Eyes up here," she signed.

Long strands of white hair covered her cleavage, and Eddison's purple eyes investigated hers. He wanted to touch her, but something bound his arms and legs. There wasn't panic, fear, or even rage—all he wanted was this woman.

"The lust will fade once the claim sets," she began.

"Claim?"

She gave him a sly smile. "All questions will be answered, but I need you to wait here until you get your body under control."

Eddison looked at her, confused. "What is a claim? What did you do to me?"

"You're a Witch in a Hellion-owned territory. Both sides want you for your blood and ability." Her hands moved quickly, but Eddison was familiar with sign language.

"Please . . . I don't understand."

"By me claiming you, no one will attack. They will sense my power, and if a Heaven-sent dares to cross into my territory again, I will be able to find them quickly."

"The Angel, what did you do to him?" Eddison asked, slowly calming down now that his questions were being answered.

Those eyes never looked away from him. Her body language showed she was comfortable. Eddison was in an unfamiliar place, but all that mattered to him was this woman, the one who had his full attention.

"He is alive, not that you should care."

When she moved away from him, Eddison panicked, but she continued to move her hands, showing she wasn't finished speaking.

"I needed to make a statement that the Angel would convey. A statement that anyone will be punished if they harmed you. Being a messenger guaranteed his life."

Her body continued to move towards the open door. This moment was when the panic started to sink in. Where was he? Who was this woman? Why was she leaving him? His mind was so overpowered by these questions that he no longer paid attention to her. All he wanted to do was leave.

"Don't leave me!" he yelled.

She frowned and stopped in the doorway, waiting until Eddison looked at her before she spoke with her hands once more. "My mother called me Dinah as a baby. A name can bring comfort in knowing you are not my captive, but I cannot trust that you won't harm yourself until the claim sets. Try and get some rest . . ."

The thoughts of having her on top of him, being able to be deep inside her, clouded his mind. Dinah. His beautiful creature had a name, and all he wanted to do was hold her. Touch her. Devour her.

*

Dinah let out a loud sigh. This was harder than she thought. Eddison's cravings were a reaction to the changes his body was experiencing. Her attention shifted from the closed door to an individual sitting at the table.

The entire apartment followed the theme of onyx and darkness. Red velvet and black leather. It was her home when she was in the Mortal world. The man at the table created comfort over fear. He moved his body to turn, and his wings, black as night, like hers, moved with him.

"How am I alive?" she signed.

Seven individuals existed that Hellions feared. Their wings were hidden in the darkest parts of Hell, so no one saw them, but the face of the man at her table was one that created nightmares.

A blindfold covered his eyes with the mark of the Hellion king sewn into the fabric, and another covered the mouth, the same as the one that Eddison removed from Dinah's body that took away her voice. An individual bred for war sat in her kitchen, but he had no plans of attacking. His true intentions fell to the woman who trusted him wholeheartedly.

"I do not know," Vadim signed in return.

Dinah walked closer to him. "The low lives had their fill, but the Demons wouldn't go near me."

"You could not have escaped on your own."

She pulled out a chair and sat across from him. "I was rotting away, but now I am not. The details do not matter."

The man before her held a power the worlds feared. They ruled armies, held the rank of general, but never did they show any weakness. The slightest advantage the enemy had would risk their victory. A weakness would mean their extinction.

"You claimed a Human, I can smell it on you."

Dinah's eyes traveled to the closed room that held Eddison. He could be screaming, and no one outside would hear him. Why did she care if he lived or died? General

Vadim did not follow her gaze; instead, he put a black cloth on the table as he stood. There was a symbol on that cloth, one like the mark on his own.

"You have served your punishment. The choice is yours."

He left the statement open-ended before disappearing, his movements quick and silent. Those with the black wings were untraceable, but they could always find each other. Dinah knew what he meant, how she had a choice to make.

Dinah gave Eddison time to calm down before she entered the room. He was looking out the window. The look of confusion still played across his face, but the smell of the food she was bringing took his attention away from the outside.

"Where am I?" Eddison demanded.

He had a chance to inspect the entire room. The walls were a dark stone, with dark wooden floors and a red rug. It was minimal but the furniture that existed within looked old. This wasn't a home for a Human, and from how bare this room truly was, he suspected Dinah didn't live here permanently.

"Eat," she signed, leaving the plate within reach.

He was bound to each bedpost, but there was enough slack that he could feed himself. The clothing Dinah changed into was comfortable for her, but it was tight on her body. The way Eddison's pupils became large the longer he looked at her made it obvious how he was feeling.

31

"By the way you are looking at me, it is obvious the effects haven't worn off."

Eddison's eyes fixed to her generous chest hidden underneath the sweater she wore.

"What did you do to me?" he demanded.

She rolled her eyes. "As I explained previously, the scent you will give off—the claim—will keep other Hellions from bothering you. The Angels will sense the power it will emanate and avoid conflict."

"What do you want from me?"

"When you leave this apartment," she signed. "You will never see me again or will ever have to worry about being attacked. Think of this as a protection from your Wiccan blood."

Dinah was getting annoyed with having to explain the same information. Rather than hear more demands from her captive, she turned to walk out, but she stopped the moment she felt contact.

Eddison was able to loosen one of his binds to get a hand released. To feel her skin, so soft and warm, made his blood boil on contact.

"I have spent my entire life helping people. It didn't matter if you were Demon or Angel. I have a life that I accepted, but when I saw you on that sacrificial post, I couldn't let you die."

It was obvious to him that Dinah was stronger. Her size did not matter. When Eddison pulled her down to him, she came willingly and didn't back away when his lips found hers.

A kiss. It ignited them both. Dinah should have pulled away. To claim an individual was for a purpose, but Dinah was tired of fighting this feeling. Vadim showed concern in her claim, but how can something that felt so right be bad?

Questions kept going through her mind. Why did she save him? Was it a moment of weakness? That weakness could disappear with the blindfold, it was a ticket back to her old life, but did she want that?

"What did you do to me?" Eddison whispered with a voice filled with lust and need.

Dinah didn't respond. All she did was slowly straddle his lap and put a hand on his chest. Her long white hair fell past her shoulders as those red eyes studied the man before her. Slowly, her hand rose once more, using the only form of communication she had.

"Eat something. Once the lust fades . . . you are free to go wherever you please."

Eddison was not satisfied with that answer. When Dinah went to move, he grabbed her thigh with his free hand.

"When I saw you on that post, it wasn't my need to help you that made me go against the rules. There was a draw, a need that I cannot put into words. I do not have to know who you are or ultimately what you did to me, Dinah. All I ask . . . is for you to kiss me again."

The moment those last words came out of Eddison's mouth, Dinah reached her fist back and punched him hard in the face. The point of contact rendered the man unconscious, giving Dinah the time to figure out how to deal with him.

IV

"Move it!" a beast snarled.

"Did you say something to me?" the other responded.

This city was unique. It was filled with the darkest and damnest of creatures, yet it was held together by respect and honor. It was why Dinah chose it as her hiding place. It was one of the few Hellion cities in the Mortal realm.

No one needed to see her face or feel her power. Her wings were the universal symbol of the power she possessed. When she stepped into the nightclub, people took one look at her and moved away. Her face was hidden underneath a hood. Her destination was a creature observing the dance floor, the owner and current caretaker of this block.

"It's her . . .," the whispers announced.

Infamous. Her power, her reign was feared not only by Angels but by those who lived in the darkness. She had two purposes: to serve and to protect. Everyone stepped back, but the individual with scales instead of skin looked at her with concern. He had the body of a Human but a head of a reptile, the hybrid that she needed to talk to.

"General," he said, but Dinah held up a finger to silence him.

"She is going to kill him."

"We need to run."

"If we do, she will kill us too."

Dinah raised her other hand, and everyone watched: "Spread the word. The Witch is under my claim and will not be harmed."

The man of scales only nodded, and everyone scrambled. They wanted nothing to do with the general or the Witch. The dim lightning faded when the remaining lights turned on. She waited until they were alone to make another point.

With a swift kick, the man fell to the ground. He knew better than to attack, but she wanted this to be known.

"I served my punishment, and I am still as powerful as before. If I hear anyone talking about me behind my back, you are the first person I will come after."

They knew how to communicate with the general. Dinah's voiceless words were understood, and the nod confirmed it. To be a sacrifice on a post was deemed an execution. It was meant to display the gruesome death to those who disobey. With word spreading that Dinah survived the sacrifice, it wouldn't be long before others sought her out. She needed to be in control, to protect Eddison.

*

Eddison chose to save a dying woman. A noble act, but he now found himself kidnapped and lusting for the woman he pieced back together. There was a pile of clothing his size near the bed and food on the bedside table

36

at every meal. She wasn't hurting him, but it was clear he was her captive.

This home was rich with material no longer available. War had destroyed natural resources that made simple items harder to find.

When he woke up, Eddison was no longer bound, and he was finally able to get out of that bed.

Fully clothed, Eddison walked out of that room and saw a large fireplace in the distance. One that held the green flames that can only be found in one place. Hell. Any denial that this could have been a dream was erased when he saw those flames.

His eyes drifted to the high ceilings above that held more hellfire trapped in glass balls. They moved effortlessly, floating with no destination in sight. It was chaos contained. When he looked at the chair in front of him, he saw Dinah watching the flames move.

"Are you going to kill me?" he asked, staying in the doorway of the bedroom.

Dinah raised her hand.

"No," she signed.

"Am I your prisoner?"

Dinah had a glass of wine in her hand. She leaned forward, placing it on the coffee table before standing. She was small yet powerful. Those magnificent black wings tucked behind her accented the black low-cut dress she wore. When Eddison took a step towards her, she raised a hand to forbid it.

"Talk to me . . .," Eddison begged.

Dinah moved her hands. "You are not my prisoner, Witch."

Eddison didn't believe her. "I am free to go?"

"As long as you stay in the city, you will be protected."

He knew better than to move from this spot. Dinah made it perfectly clear he was not to advance, but this was the first time she was honest with him.

"This house you can use as you wish," she added.

Eddison growled. "Why am I here? Why me?"

The growl came from a deep part of his throat. An animalistic noise that gave him the courage to take a step forward. That action caused Dinah to smirk. A Witch can do many things, and the stronger the blood, the stronger the Witch. There was a seal on Eddison's back, one that Dinah noticed the moment she removed his clothing. She thought it contained his magic, but when her wine glass flew into the fire, she understood she was mistaken.

"Tell me!" he snapped as she raised a hand, pushing Eddison against the wall with the power of energy.

Moving to him, his eyes bore into the soulless body she held. "You can demand nothing from me, Witch."

When Eddison went to speak again, the darkness covered his mouth. Those violet eyes glared at her, and she heard more glass breaking in the distance. Sharp shards flew towards Dinah, but a cutting board caught them before they got close.

"Let me go or kill me."

Dinah now held a playful smile. No one challenged her and lived. She almost was looking forward to what he would try to do.

"You saved my life, an act that will cost you. Never take down a sacrifice."

With each movement of her hands, Dinah got closer. The darkness moved away from Eddison when she was within arm's reach. It gave Eddison back his voice.

"I will never apologize for saving you. It doesn't matter who or what you are—"

"By you saving me, I am bound to save you. A debt for a debt. My protection goes as far as this city. If you choose to go beyond it, you will be on your own."

Eddison couldn't look away from her or escape the lewd thoughts that plagued his mind. His magic was never a thing he chose to use for his own benefit. It can be sensed, tracked, and create a greater target on his back. Manipulating the air around him was harmless, but when Eddison was pinned by her darkness, his violet eyes flared.

He vanished and appeared behind her. The darkness was attuned to Dinah, but the light that Eddison appeared from she could track. But the general wasn't fast enough because Eddison was able to pin her to the ground at his feet.

The light that came from his body touched her, but it didn't harm her. Those born of darkness reject the light, but Dinah did not struggle. It surprised them both.

"I am holding your hands, taking away your ability to communicate so you will listen to me," Eddison began, aware of the hounds that circled him.

He interlocked his fingers with hers, making sure she understood that she needed to listen. "I am not a tool for the Hellions to use. All my life I have been serving the world as a healer. Never once discriminated by species. I treated everyone fairly."

Dinah licked her lips, distracting Eddison only for a moment. "It is my job to heal, and you were dying. I will not apologize for saving you, and you owe me no debt. Let me go, Dinah . . . please."

When Eddison let her hands go, he continued to hover above her. Rather than speak, Dinah raised her hand to prevent the hounds from interfering. Once they were truly alone, she reached up and touched his face.

"You had a block down your throat that prevented you from talking. Your vocal cords are intact, you can speak to me . . ."

Eddison stopped his thought process when she caused him to grow hard. It rubbed up against her, but rather than push him away, she reached behind his neck, pulling him down. The moment her lips met his, she opened her mouth, inviting Eddison to finally get what he wanted.

Dinah would never admit to him that a part of her, the one that the blindfold would suppress, wanted him. To claim an individual in Hell meant something that he could never understand. The feelings he felt, she felt them too.

Her hands turned into claws, slowly ripping off his shirt and gently scratching his muscular chest. A moan escaped his lips, and he lifted her dress. His body shivered when Eddison realized she wasn't wearing anything underneath.

Breaking the kiss only for a moment, he lifted her and brought her into the bedroom. Her black wings were soft against his arms, not hard or sharp like they were when she was attacking.

Desire. It never hit Eddison like this. His hand found where he wanted to go, and he got her ready. She moved underneath him, making little sounds to show she could indeed talk if she wanted. She was incredible.

"You are beautiful," he whispered to her.

Pure instinct took over and they both listened to their bodies. When they joined, they both shivered at the feeling. It was more than they both imagined it would be. The need was raw, and that scream turned into pleasureful noises when Eddison moved.

Her body responded to his thrusts by having her wings wrap around him, protecting them both during this intimate moment. When they both hit their peak, they released in sync, and their bodies hummed until they both fell asleep tightly in each other's embrace.

*

Eddison didn't know how much time had passed, but when he woke up, his body still hummed. It took him a moment to remember that he was a captive in this room. Something warm was wrapped against him. It was her wings, keeping him warm as they both slept. She was still here, with him, sharing the bed.

But his smile in seeing her there turned into a frown when he saw her exposed back. Her skin was flawless except around her joints where the wings came out of her back. Old scars from whippings were hidden, only to be revealed as she breathed in and out. This woman, his woman, was tortured.

His woman? Why would Eddison think Dinah was his? That thought scared him.

When he climbed out of the bed, he made sure she still slept as he got dressed.

Eddison didn't have time till now to look around the apartment. It was old, and each artifact on display seemed ancient. The stone was cold but the green flame in the hearth warmed the entire room.

The kitchen was simple and modernized over the rest of the apartment. A long couch in front of the fire was the only furniture aside from the table. It was empty of anything that seemed personal.

"What did you do to me?" Eddison asked calmly once more, turning to see Dinah standing in the bedroom doorway.

"You saved my life when no one would. For that I grant you safe passage in this city, and as a reward, I will give you the gift you desire most."

Eddison raised an eyebrow. "Desire?"

"Your belongings are in the chests. If you need any Wiccan materials for your rituals, write me a list."

He watched her move towards the kitchen. "I am not your prisoner, yet I can't leave this city. For saving your life, you will give me what I desire most?"

Dinah only nodded. When Eddison walked up to her and put his hand on her face, she didn't turn away. Those red eyes looked at him with a longing he too felt, but Eddison could swear there was a vulnerability in those

42

eyes as well. One she was so afraid to show, and he swore at that moment that he would protect it, even if she didn't need it. He was not leaving this city now that he had found someone he wanted.

V

The lust should have only lasted forty-eight hours, but it had been weeks since the claim and the feelings were still there. It was constant. Over and over, they fed into their desires, not once thinking about what this could mean.

Even though the invisible chains existed on Eddison, the longer he stayed with Dinah, the less he fought to leave. He had so many questions for her, but he refrained from asking because a part of him was afraid to know the answers.

When Eddison ventured out of the apartment, no one gave him any trouble. The whispers started about a claimed Witch. Claimed. That word was defined the moment he found a bookstore, thankful for knowing many Hellion languages.

To claim an individual was a form of mating. Individuals from Hell marked their prey and chose them to create life and strengthen their ranks. It talked about a forced corruption, but his time with Dinah was never forced.

Never once was Eddison stopped from coming and going, but when they happened to be in the same room, they found themselves entangled in each other's arms hours later. Was she using him to create life? If so, why him? But after all that he read, the why slowly was becoming irrelevant.

"You have questions," Eddison observed when she sat down next to him, looking at the book he was reading.

"As do you," she signed.

"Who goes first?"

Dinah took the book carefully out of his hand and put it aside. "You."

Eddison shifted so he was looking at her. "Are you using me for my magical bloodline?"

"I am not, nor will I ever use you, Eddison. The claim was to protect you within this city from other Hellions who want you for your Wiccan blood."

"But you are carrying my child?" he asked.

It all made sense. They were not using protection, and he never thought about the consequences of their actions. He was too consumed in the pleasure, but the motivation was clear. If she was trying to get pregnant, he wouldn't stop her.

"You desire to be loved. A child will love you unconditionally, and you will love it in return. This is my gift to you, as a thank you for saving my life."

In her telling him this, Eddison had to pause. He was trying to understand what she was saying. She got pregnant, for him. Not to advance her species or rank as the book said, but to give him something he could love.

"The draw I felt towards you, Dinah, was before you claimed me," Eddison began, taking her hand in his.

"I know you do not believe that you are only doing this to give me a child. You do not bring a child into this world every time someone saves you. There is something more, something you are not telling me."

Dinah did not respond; all she did was hold onto his hand tightly and rest her head on his body. A claim lasted only forty-eight hours, long enough for impregnation, but the feeling, the one that they both shared, still lingered, and it terrified her.

"I know you care for me as I do you. Words cannot always express a feeling, Dinah, but I do not care who or what you did to become a sacrifice. All that matters to me is the here and now. Our child is a start for the both of us, one we will both take. Please, Dinah, let me know you feel the same as I do."

She couldn't say it, her mind wouldn't let her. How she clung onto him showed Eddison she did feel the same way. She was expected to be strong. If she had a weakness, it could kill her, but he would spend however long it took to show that he and this child were not a weakness but an asset in assuring her a happy future.

*

Her belly grew as the months passed, but what Dinah did when she left the house, Eddison would never know. The one moment of feeling they shared that day was the only time she was ever vulnerable. Dinah needed to be cold to exert her power; it was the only way the creatures of this city would leave them alone.

46

"Are you a doctor?" the older creature asked the moment Eddison knelt in front of her.

He always seemed to find those in need. It didn't matter what they were or who they claimed as their leader, he treated them all the same. Gently, Eddison wrapped her hoofed foot after treating the open wound only a few moments prior.

"I am," he began.

"Why are you helping me? I do not have any money."

He looked up to the Demon. She was afraid of him; a lot of individuals knew who he was claimed by and stayed away. But, when he showed them kindness, that fear slowly started to disappear and the need for his services was revealed.

"Make sure you go to the hospital, this will need stitches to prevent it from reopening,"

His magic was dulled with the Hellions around him, but in the apartment, his home, that block was not there. Many sought to challenge Eddison, to try and see why he was claimed over someone else. It was a challenge a few dared to attempt, but when they did, he watched them fall to the ground lifeless. No one had been able to successfully execute their threats against him.

Dinah walked up to them, and she raised her hand. Those lifeless bodies consumed in the green flames of Hell vanished from existence permanently.

The woman crawled away from Eddison in fear. The sight of Dinah, a Hellion general, made everyone consumed by fear. They never got a chance to know the woman he had fallen for, the one that was carrying his child and the one he couldn't deny that he loved with all his heart.

"You were due back ten minutes ago," she signed.

"We've talked about this," Eddison spoke with anger on his face.

Dinah rolled her eyes. "I am a soldier, Eddison, I will never change."

She still refused to speak, but there was never a barrier in communication. Eddison focused on her face when she signed. His peripheral vision made it so he could read her signs and still focus on those ruby eyes.

"The fetus will remain unharmed as we agreed," she added.

Eddison didn't respond, he only walked up to her and touched her growing stomach. He hated that she was trying to disconnect from the child, afraid to feel love. He tried time and time again to tell her that this was their child, but nothing he said would change her mind. Words meant nothing to a person who lived a life of war, actions are what got through to them, and he knew, when it was time for this child to come out, she would change.

Her wings wrapped around him, making Eddison look into those eyes. She leaned in, kissing him without caring if someone saw. Emotion. She couldn't show it, but he could feel it in every kiss. A need. She was screaming on the inside, but until she told him what she needed, Eddison could only be here for her, to catch her when she fell apart.

*

"You need to breathe."

The months ticked by until Eddison was woken up early one morning to the sound of Dinah trying to suppress a scream. Her body was shaking as the contractions came closer and closer. The pain was from the inside. She wanted to rip the child out, to stop it from happening.

"Dinah—"

Her robe was wet from her water breaking. Ripping off what little clothing she had gave her a moment of satisfaction. She glared at him and raised her hands to speak in the only way she felt comfortable.

"Get. It. Out!"

Her movements were fast and sluggish. The groan she tried to suppress slipped from her mouth as another contraction snuck up on her. It hurt. She wanted this pain to stop, and Eddison stayed at her side, trying to soothe her.

"Your body is doing what it needs to do. I need you to let it happen," he moved some hair out of her face.

"It hurts . . .," she managed to sign.

"I am right here."

Their relationship changed the moment their son came into the world, a moment that caused her to let out another pain-filled groan, allowing their daughter to follow closely behind. Once she was cleaned up and calm, Eddison gave her the children, her babies.

The look she gave them showed the love she had for them. It was a love she tried to deny herself the entire time she was pregnant, but she no longer fought it. Both of their children had a small mass of red hair on their heads and eyes that glistened the moment they looked at their mother. They were not red like hers; they were purple like Eddison's but still shimmered like a jewel.

"They are beautiful . . ." she hoarsely spoke.

Her words, the first words he ever heard her speak felt like a song to his ears. It was pure joy that made him yearn to hear it again. It created a sense of hope and joy in his being. One that he wanted to never forget. Eddison leaned down and kissed the top of her head gently.

"Like their mother."

Eddison never thought he would ever be a father. The notion of children was never on his mind. He needed to survive but seeing the two bundles in the arms of the woman he learned to love, he didn't want them to get taken away.

"They need names," Eddison whispered.

Dinah laid both children on the bed in front of her, allowing them to wiggle out of the blanket Eddison swaddled them in. She watched as their daughter was the first to kick the blanket away, and it caused her to smile.

"Nova . . .," she whispered.

"Our son?"

Dinah watched the boy. He was content in the blanket, unlike his sister. He was calm while she was full of movement. "Kace . . ."

They were a family. One that never would have come into being if Eddison left her on that post. But he stayed by Dinah's side. Even when she refused to allow her children

50

out of arm's reach, he knew that protectiveness was a form of the love she felt for them. One he was afraid she would never be able to express.

Her body healed at a rapid rate. If it wasn't for Eddison, her basic needs would have been forgotten because her focus was on her children. They had small, featherless wings on their backs that she treated with the utmost care. She told him that these children were a gift so he would have someone to love, but Eddison quickly realized that she needed someone too, and in a sense, they both got a family.

The next few days she only spoke when she was talking to the babies. They responded to her voice with loving eyes and playful sounds. She bathed them, fed them from her breasts, and made sure they always smiled. Those few days were the happiest she ever had, but as quickly as that happiness formed, a Hellion army descended onto her city.

Eddison woke up to a cold bed and screaming newborns. "Dinah?"

Panic shot through him when he looked around their room and couldn't find her. Dinah was always in the same room as the children, never allowed them to be out of her sight. Jumping out of bed, he heard a noise outside the building and looked out the window.

Dinah was standing before the massive army in nothing more than a black dress. Her wings were not in an attack position, and her body seemed calm. But what worried him most was the blindfold in her hand.

"Your king gave you a year as a reward for surviving your punishment," a soldier said.

51

There was no leader because this was an escort. That soldier was here to deliver a message, and he looked at Dinah with no fear. Which meant that they knew of her and what caused her to get to this place in her life.

"That year is up, General. I have come to collect you on His Majesty's order."

Eddison rushed out of the apartment, his pulse racing. He was going to lose her—that statement kept running over and over through his head. Rather than getting close to the woman he loved, he hit an invisible wall.

Dinah did not respond to the soldier, but she took a few steps forward. An individual appeared in front of her, his wings spread high and wide. Wings of black, like Dinah's, presented for all to see. His eyes covered by the same blindfold she held in her hand, and the face mask was familiar to Eddison too. His white hair was long and held back in a braid. It was a display, a presentation of power. His body was encased in black metal, a uniform of one of the Seven Generals of Hell.

Dinah looked at that man and then lowered her head in defeat. It was then it all clicked for Eddison. General. He knew that the rank of general floated around Dinah. The white hair, black wings. He felt that it was part of her race but looking to the man and seeing how much they were similar, he knew she wasn't just any general.

Eddison was so blinded by the need to protect her that he failed to acknowledge what he knew: she evoked fear in everything she touched. Dinah was one of them. When she finally looked in Eddison's direction, she signed one more thing before she vanished:

"Protect them."

VI

Twenty Years Later

The moment the sun fell, and the moon rose, the last Hellion city came alive. The population had tripled as the years progressed. When you have individuals struggling to survive, they will also fight for power.

Poverty. Gangs. Violence. It was the way of life. If you didn't join a gang or have some influence, you wouldn't last a year, let alone twenty. But those two little babes grew up in the community, and rather than wither away and die, they thrived.

Eddison knew their mother's influence was still around, but people forgot who he was to her. It was a gift in surviving this city, but it didn't prevent his children from being consumed by their surroundings.

"Sir, he is here . . ."

A horned man sat at the bar, looking to the patrons before him. When the server spoke, the man tensed. It was the one man that everyone made sure to stay on his good side.

"Make sure he is pleased," he responded.

The nightclub pounded with music that bounced off the walls and floor. Lights illuminated every dark place so no one could hide. Bodies moved all around, but one person was still, almost like a stone as he watched the world before him.

He was tall and always wore dark clothing to conceal himself. His hood was down, and bright red hair was all anyone saw. It was unreal, brighter than anyone had ever seen, but it matched the color of his father's.

"Is there anything else I can get you?" a woman asked.

She wore tight leather clothing and her tail wrapped around her leg. All the workers use their sex appeal to get tips, but the man with a symbol of death and pain on his back never looked.

He said nothing, only motioned for her to leave. His attention was on a woman who was dancing in a large group. Her long black ballgown clung to her. It was low cut, and it not only revealed her bosom but also a large tattoo across her chest.

The man growled. No one dared to go near her, but that red curly hair moved wildly. She was all over the dance floor, loving the attention. He looked at every individual that approached, not minding the person that slowly sat down beside him.

"How long?" he asked.

His voice was deep, but there was an underlying sound that seemed to draw in everyone around him. The new man was large and made the redheaded individual seem small in comparison.

"Till she turns twenty—"

The redhead didn't like that answer. "I want more time."

The man was larger, over six foot eight, all muscle. His hair glistened a golden hue that matched the eyes watching the woman out on the dance floor. His dark suit was the man's way of blending in, but everyone saw him sitting next to the most feared hitman in the city, and by association, feared him too.

"Twenty."

The hitman leaned forward. "I am still uncomfortable with this arrangement."

The woman appeared behind them, leaning over the couch. She wrapped her arms around the large man with golden hair and smiled. She showed no fear in those jeweled irises. Even when she climbed over the couch and into his lap, she looked over to the smaller man, the one with the same face as her.

There was no denying that they were twins. The female swung her legs into her brother's lap. He was the man with the symbol of fear and pain on his back. It was then the blades strapped to her thigh revealed to show that she was more than a pretty face.

"Why are you bothering my husband?" she asked.

When her brother went to speak, she brought her heeled boot up to his face. There was a blade hidden underneath that heel, one that she could use at any time. The awkward position she now found herself in revealed more of her skin than he would have liked.

The large man with the golden hair slowly put her leg down and pulled the fabric back over her skin. He was protective of what was his, and this woman was always going to be his, no matter what her brother claimed.

"Mate, not husband."

His sister glared at him. "Watch your mouth!"

"It is not your fault his Dragon ass is mated to your soul."

The words her brother spoke were true. She wanted to be mad at him, but she knew it was all because he cared. But she was not going to let him get away from insulting the one she called her husband, regardless of the circumstances.

"Don't push me, Kace," she muttered.

The man known as Kace smirked. "Try me, Nova."

Kace. Nova. Their life was nothing but ordinary compared to others in this city. They had to do what was needed to survive. Everything fell into place except those jeweled irises they always hid behind sunglasses. It wasn't because of the glimmer but the Wiccan blood that flowed through their veins, a characteristic passed down by their father.

"You do realize this whole mate thing doesn't fall on you because you are not a Dragon!"

"Because I don't—"

Kace quickly stood, losing his composure. "You are not thinking!"

Nova watched him walk out of the club and sighed. Everyone feared her brother, but he got flustered when things didn't go his way. Rather than talk about it like an adult, he would storm off like a toddler trying to find the upper hand before advancing for a second attack.

"Don't provoke him," the large man said.

Nova didn't take her husband's warning. She jumped out of his lap and found her way out of the club. She knew that she was being watched, but if anyone dared to approach, Nova could take care of herself.

"You are mad that I found someone," Nova whispered when she caught up to Kace.

Her brother raised his hands in defeat. "He marked you."

That part of his statement was true. The mark on her chest was that of the Dragon's. It was worn with pride but also as a warning that if anyone dared to hurt her, there would be a winged beast coming after them.

"It wasn't his—"

Kace refused to allow her to speak. "He marked you when you were a child!"

That defeated expression vanished quickly, but Nova refused to back down.

"I may have accidently wondered into his realm, but that doesn't mean he doesn't care about me!"

They both stopped in front of a familiar building, one that they had called home all their lives, as the argument continued.

"I do not care of his scaley politics, you are Human!"

"You are mad that he makes me happy!"

"I thought I made you happy!" Kace finally admitted.

She scoffed. "Is that what this is? Are you jealous that he will have more time than you? You are my brother, Kace, and I will always love you, but I am growing up—"

Kace wasn't ready to have this conversation. Even though they were only a few minutes apart, he always acted like he was the older one. "Come on. If I am going to have three months left with you, I might as well not make it difficult."

Nova watched him walk up those familiar stairs and frowned. It was not supposed to be this hard. They were a family, but she understood. It had been the three of them for twenty years, and now that she was leaving, he will be all alone.

Their home used to be a single apartment, but as they grew up, the entire complex was carved into a house. When they both entered, the green orbs floated above their heads, a familiar and comforting sight.

When they were small, their father spoke of a time they would try to catch them. Hellfire was unstable, and the flame couldn't be put out unless it could be controlled. Their father created an endless space above their heads for the orbs to travel. He didn't want to get rid of them but also didn't want to risk curious children getting hurt.

"Father agreed with your mating because Navar is the King of Dragons. His Wiccan—"

Kace couldn't help himself. He had to get the last word. The open layout made it easy for the twins to find their space, to feel free over trapped, but as they grew older, the volume of their arguments did not get quieter.

"I can summon Dragons, Kace."

"I know that—"

She shook her head, walking towards the kitchen. "It is a power no Witch possesses. If it were not for Navar helping me with my magic, I could have lost control."

Kace stayed in the distance but was not done with this conversation. "You were a child—"

"And he treated me respectfully till I was of age. I love him, Kace . . . Why can't you see that?"

Nova was honest in her question, but rather than facing a conversation he knew he couldn't win, Kace walked up the spiral staircase towards his room. They both mumbled not-so-nice words under their breaths, matching the frustration they both felt.

*

Both twins flourished in those years. Eddison did all he could to support them, but it was the city that made them who they were today. Walking into his home, the doctor heard the grumbling of his two children and sighed.

Even though Dinah had been missing their entire lives, the protection she promised had stayed. He spent all his time with his children, homeschooling them while teaching them the fundamentals of their magic. But there was a part he couldn't prepare them for: the Hellion part that they explored without his watchful eye.

"Do I dare ask?" he asked his daughter.

She didn't answer him at first. Nova knew better than to have on such a revealing dress in front of her father, so she'd changed into a sweater and jeans. Grumbling into the stew, she slowly looked over to the man who was her whole world and didn't know where to start.

"You can talk to me, Nova," Eddison said calmly.

"You like Navar, right?"

Eddison only gave her a small smile. This conversation had been happening a lot recently, ever since the Dragon king asked her to marry him. Eddison was calm, but it was his son that caused all the frustration.

"It isn't funny!" Nova called out.

Eddison put his workbag down. "I never said it was."

Nova was gifted with an ancient ability. There was a time when she was a small child that he almost lost her, but Navar, he protected her. That protection became a friendship, and when she was of age, a courtship. Eddison trusted his intentions but would never admit it when Kace was against the idea. He refused to choose sides.

"Father!" she snapped as Kace came down the stairs.

"Did you pick up my package from the market?" Eddison asked his son.

He was happy to change the subject, but he frowned when Kace reached for his boots. He was not blind to his son's reputation. What he did wasn't something Eddison could judge him for, but he feared for his safety. Even though his son was nineteen, they were in different parts of this city, ones that each could not cross without repercussions. Kace taking his packages created a greater divide between father and son.

"In your room," Kace replied, leaving the house.

Eddison needed to smuggle in Heaven-sent ingredients to treat some of the injured. They were forbidden in a Hellion city, but his son made sure they got through. This family was not perfect, but it worked. Even if it felt like they were drifting further apart.

*

Kace was feared and respected, but what he kept from his family was to prevent their judgement. What he did was to protect them, but they didn't need to know the details. It wasn't the first time a few Heaven-sent individuals were found looking for a Witch in the Hellion city, but it was the first time one was stupid enough to try again.

"I do not understand!"

Dozens of men lined the walls in the abandoned warehouse, all with the same confused expression. "By keeping the Angel alive, it will draw more to our location!"

"It is not in our best interest to judge him."

The loud one scoffed. "I am not going to get killed over a dumb—"

When Kace entered the warehouse, all talking ceased. His eyes were not on his men, who were waiting for the next command, but on the Angel who was sitting quietly in the center of the vacant spot.

Wings of white bent and broken in many directions. Chains were holding him down, digging into his flesh to guarantee his compliance. His light-colored hair was

S. G. Blinn

stained with dirt and blood, with a dirty rag covering his eyes.

His breathing was steady. Regardless of the beating he faced, the Angel was prepared for more. This one was different. Rather than looking blindly around the city, he went directly to the hospital, as if knowing where the Witch would be. Kace had traps to protect his father, but for this Angel to bypass all of them made the need to question him a higher priority than setting an example.

"Sir—"

Kace raised his hand to silence the fool who dared to speak to him. This Angel held a power he hadn't seen before. He was strong enough to kill twelve of his men before they got him under control. Taking a few steps forward, Kace made sure his hood was up before he spoke.

"You are a brave soul to invade a Hellion city," he spoke.

There was a mask on Kace's face distorting his voice. There was something about his and Nova's voices that created a draw to all who listened. It was faint but it caused enough problems that when he was working, he needed to hide it.

"Do you speak?" Kace asked.

Yellow blood dripped from his head when he raised it towards Kace's voice. Blood can be an indication of race, with yellow being Angelic and black Hellion, but Kace was more focused on the lack of worry that seemed to cross the Angel's face. When the Angel didn't speak, Kace punched him hard across the face.

62

He spat blood out of his mouth. "I seek not to strike any ill will with you."

His voice was strong but another strike from Kace made it obvious the time for a drawn-out talk was over.

"Wrong answer," Kace growled.

"I speak the truth—"

Another punch to the face. "Why are you here!"

The Angel accepted every punch and waited till Kace drew his fist back before speaking.

"I have come to guide my charge out of harm."

Charge. It was a term used by guardian Angels. It made sense now why this one was so strong, but to avoid a fight almost made Kace disappointed. He hadn't had a good opponent in years.

"No creature lives in this city that requires assistance from your kind . . ."

It wasn't till marks appeared on the floor and slowly crawled up the Angel's leg that he became worried. That stoic expression turned to concern, but it was too late. Those markings prevented the Angel from moving only temporarily, which was enough time for Kace to get closer.

"I know your rule—"

Kace refused to let him speak. He picked him up, the bindings falling to the floor. Kace had a power, one that he showed often to declare dominance, but the Angel was still in shock that he possessed a power no Hellion creature had the capability of having. A power to cast magic.

"I am done talking with you. Give me the name of your charge!" Kace demanded.

The Angel was weak. Kace's men had beat him long enough to make him compliant before Kace got involved, but rather than agree to his demands, the Angel grabbed Kace's wrist and squeezed.

"The war is rising to a turning point. If the mortals do not choose a side, they will perish. You have no mortal Human or Angelic loyal in your city, but with so much mixed blood, can you truly track everyone?"

Angelic. Hellion. Mortal. It did not matter the blood to determine the victor. Kace was known to be fair yet stern. No one worried about one side buying his affection. He was the only neutral force left in this city, a position that came with its own level of complications.

"You will be brought to the border and released," he began.

It was against his better judgement, but he needed the Angel to send a message.

"This is your final warning, Angel. If you or anyone else cross, I will show no mercy."

Kace dropped him hard on the ground before the Angel decided to speak again. "You cover yourself well, young one, more than most, but there is one flaw in your tactics. That single piece will be your downfall. Do you care to learn what it is?"

Kace did not have time for this. He turned his body and started to walk away. A single Angel was no threat, and he still had time to fix the traps, but the moment he heard *his* name, Kace froze.

"Dr. Eddison is being targeted by the Hellions. He still refuses to choose a side, but he needs to gain the protection needed to survive. I know you're protecting him—"

Kace took a deep breath, turning back to the Angel. Rather than beat him senseless, with a quick click of his phone, he took a picture of his face before giving his henchmen the freedom to do with the Angel as they pleased. The name. His father's name, how did the Angel know it?

*

Kace didn't stay out long. When he returned home, he saw his father in the living room working on the charts he'd brought home from work.

"Where is Nova?" he asked.

His sister adored their father; he could do no wrong in her eyes. If he chose a side, Kace would no longer be able to protect him. He watched him working hard for creatures that would tear him apart if they didn't have a use for him. The man was always working, but also found time for his children. How was he supposed to talk to him about the guardian Angel?

"Father?"

Eddison didn't look up from his papers. "She went out."

Eddison was expecting his son to say something else, so when he didn't, Eddison looked up. There was something troubling him. Regardless of how well Kace thought he could hide his emotions, a father always knew.

The nineteen-year-old looked defeated and those purple eyes showed anxiety. He motioned to the chair beside him, and Kace took it without reservation.

"There is a fine line between us, Kace."

"I know," Kace replied.

"It is one created against my wishes, but it was needed for this family to survive. I had to make choices that I am not proud of, but I did it so you and your sister could be safe."

Kace lowered his head. "It isn't fair . . ."

"I know," Eddison began, putting a hand on his son's shoulder.

"We either must work against the system or allow it to strengthen us. Like Nova: events took place to shape her into the woman she is growing to be. It doesn't matter how I feel about Navar and his Dragon practices, I know he will protect my daughter and love her as she deserves. I wish that for you, a happiness that may not be here but out there. I do not want you to trouble yourself with me."

Kace reached for his father's hand and held onto it tightly. They were always big and strong, covered in scars from a past he refused to talk about. This city was never kind to them, but Eddison was right, it made them stronger. Kace refused to let the Angel take the one man that meant everything to him.

VII

The words kept playing through his mind the entire night. Kace couldn't rest knowing that if his father chose the Angels over the Hellions, he couldn't stay in the city. The balance needed to be kept. Kace never made an exception, even for his own father. It was frustrating and it didn't have an easy answer.

A seal rested on Kace's back. He rarely didn't have a shirt on, but in bed, he chose the least amount of fabric. It wasn't a birthmark, but his sister had one too. They couldn't find the markings in any textbook, and their father refused to tell them why they held it. The twins suspected he placed it on them, but it hadn't stopped them from doing what they wanted, so they never questioned.

"Talk to me," Nova whispered.

They gave each other space, but Kace's face drew his sister in. She crawled onto the bed and fell on top of him. His body was riddled with scars, but she never saw what was on the surface. His sister was always in tune with how he was feeling. Kace hated it, but deep down, it was a small comfort that he feared he was losing when she went to live with Navar in a few months.

"In a few months you will be crowned the Queen of the Dragons, and your life will no longer be yours."

Nova wanted to argue, but Kace was worried about something else. So, she would wait until he spoke what he needed to, to bring that light she loved about her brother. A light keeping her from going into the darkest places.

"His people will become your people, and our world will no longer be a part of who you are. I cannot accept, nor do I approve you leaving me—"

"This isn't about me, is it?" she asked gently.

Kace didn't reply. His face was her face and seeing that mark of the Dragon across her chest boiled his blood. When he went to yell, Nova hugged him, holding her brother close. Family. There was no stronger bond, but when he let out a sigh of defeat, Nova smirked.

"I made breakfast."

Kace returned the embrace. "It is still early."

"It is never too early for a home-cooked meal, come on."

Nova wiggled out of his embrace and ran towards the door. Usually, they both fought to get to the stairs, so when Kace wasn't his playful self, she frowned.

"Where is father?" he asked.

"Already left for work. He said he will be home in two days."

The city was vast, and it took days to get from one side to the other. With public transportation making it easier to move, it went from two days to six hours, but it meant he was spending a couple days at the hospital.

Thinking about his father working at the hospital made Kace remember that Angel. If he came close to him, that Angel was dead. He couldn't stand the thought of his father

68

being hurt. Breakfast would have to wait. Kace had to see if he was safe for himself.

"Where are you going?" Nova called out as her brother ran down the stairs.

"I need to check on something," he replied, getting dressed as he walked.

"Oh no, you don't!" Nova waved a spoon in the air.

"This is serious—"

Kace didn't have a chance to plead his case, Nova was already in his face. She was dressed but studying his face. Putting the spoon gently on the table, she reached for her boot, forgetting all about the meal she prepared only moments ago.

"You are not coming . . .," Kace growled.

Nova scoffed. "I am connected to the Dragon king and my magic is stronger than yours. Tell me what is going on . . . now!"

Kace pulled on his overcoat, but right beside his was a similar one for Nova. She didn't wear his symbol but watching her dress identically to him felt good. They used to be a team in the early years before her mate found out what she was doing.

"This is my city, too, brother. I may not be protecting it anymore, but that doesn't mean I don't have your back."

Side by side they stood, and Kace nodded. When they walked out of the apartment with their hoods raised, everyone refused to go near them. Kace and Nova dressed identically. Everyone knew of the twins with the connection to the Dragons. It was no secret; even though

Nova didn't wear her husband's symbol on her clothing, those who could see her skin knew the power she held.

"Don't look at them," a mother whispered.

"Mommy—"

Walking onto the subway, the crowd still parted when they moved. The smells and sounds of the busy city were familiar, and the people on this subway car were all heading in the same direction. It was a hospital vehicle, one guarded and had little crime. Hellions took care of their own, regardless of what other races thought.

Nova's eyes fell to the children. Playful, curious, and made a wonderful addition to this world. It was the newborn in their mother's arm that Kace saw her looking at. Even though he couldn't see her face, he knew the longing she had for it.

"You will make a wonderful mother," he whispered.

"I often wonder why she chose to leave . . ."

They didn't talk about their own mother much. As they got older, they were afraid to ask their father for the truth. Did they want to know the reason she left? Did she even love them?

"Father never lied to us, yet he refuses to tell us the whole truth," Kace replied.

Nova shrugged. "She left us to save us, but what could be out there that we do not already face here?"

When Kace stayed silent, Nova refused to look at him.

"He is in danger. That is the reason you couldn't sleep last night . . .," she added.

Kace didn't answer, all he did was keep his eyes forward. Mortals were here amongst the Hellions, claims

70

to spawn the next generation. They had a purpose and would rarely be seen more than once, but they were a dying race. To survive in this world, blood was needed. The weakest would suffer, and sadly, the mortals were the ones who would perish.

*

The hours ticked by, and they reached their destination, the Hellion hospital. It was split into four parts to better aid all who inhabit this city. It was no secret Dr. Eddison was in their employment, a Wiccan doctor who pledged no loyalty.

They trusted him because of that neutrality, but it could get him killed. He kept his work and private life separate; no one knew he had children. The red hair on top of Kace and Nova's heads was assumed Hellion, but their true origin was always a mystery people wanted to solve.

"We are here to see Dr. Eddison," Kace said to the woman at the receptionist's desk.

The Demon looked up and saw two identical faces hidden behind sunglasses and hoods. Fear crossed her face, knowing what it meant to see the twins. Bowing her head, she trembled.

Nova reached forward to the directory and found what they wanted. "Let's go."

Everyone was part of the Hellion race. Humans no longer worked here. It wasn't the twin's strength that made them bring fear, it was their stories and unexplained abilities. What they did not understand, people feared. It was the way it always had been.

"Patient had major blood loss due to blunt-force trauma. By the time he reached the hospital, it was too late," a doctor reported to Eddison as both men stood over a deceased body.

"Shall we investigate?"

Eddison shook his head. "Have an autopsy to determine the weapon, but the local authorities will investigate."

The doctor working under Eddison did not question. Many eager individuals wanted to work with the man, but when the doctor turned, he was face-to-face with the twins. He froze. It was the same reaction everyone gave.

The man didn't say a word; he ran down the hallway, leaving Eddison defenseless. It put a sour taste in both of his children's mouths. As their father continued taking notes, the nurses noticed the twins walk into the room and they too ran away.

"What do I owe the pleasure of your company?" he asked calmly, not looking towards them.

Eddison made sure to show no indication of the connection to the people in front of him, but before Kace could speak, the entire hospital shook. Nova took a step forward, but another shock caused the power to flicker.

"I need everyone to remain calm!" security yelled from the hallway.

It took only a moment before the window near their father shattered. The glass showered the room. Eddison's first instinct was to get to his children, but a wave of power created a distorted shield of dust, glass, and debris.

Instant. The attack happened in an instant. Their father was there one moment, and the next, he was gone. The alarms faded in chaos. Kace took a single step forward when he could see and saw a single white feather in place of where his father once stood.

"Kace?" Nova asked.

An explosion filled the entire room. The moment after he heard his sister call out to him, his ears rang. Boom. Boom. Boom. One after another until the ground beneath their feet was no more. There was a shift, a feeling that someone who didn't belong invaded what was theirs. The Angels, they were planning this from the start and waited till everyone was in one place before they made their grand gesture.

VIII

The news kept reporting the attack; it was all everyone seemed to talk about.

"The Angels have attacked the Hellion city. Eyewitness accounts have placed them surrounding the hospital that had a death toll in the thousands. Coordinately, separate attacks were spread across the city, making rescue efforts delayed. It was a massacre, more than this city has seen in over ten years."

Kace's entire body ached. The sound of the news in the distance woke him from his slumber. A strong smell filled the room, one that he was unfamiliar with, but when he tried to open his eyes, he could not.

A panic started to rise, but a hand reached out to try and calm him.

"Your eyes were severely burned. You need to let the medicine stay on for them to heal properly."

The voice that spoke was gentle. It was followed by soft hands, but the touch was unfamiliar, and it didn't calm that panic.

"Where am I?" Kace struggled to say.

"You are safe—"

Kace coughed, trying to speak louder. "I need—"

"The spell should be calming to a Hellion," a second voice added.

With the rise in panic, a pain slowly seeped in. It started on his skin and dug its way deeper. It hurt. Tiny needle pricks that were on fire. Kace tried to hold back the scream, but it forced its way out.

"He shouldn't be in pain," the gentle voice whispered.

"Get the elder!"

Movement was heard all around him, but that gentle hand refused to let him go. Acid now was running through his body on top of the stabbing, and he wanted it all to end. Kace never felt this pain before. Even though pain was a part of his life, the agony of this new sensation was too much to bear.

Another voice entered the room, one that held wisdom and a hint of fear.

"Impossible . . .," she whispered.

That pain went from immediate to dull. It consumed his being, then faded into the background. Kace had no idea how much time had passed, but when he finally was able to open his eyes, he looked up above it. Yellow greeted him.

It was a cloth stretched over a canopy bed, in gentle shades of yellow and gold. It was warm and comforting. The entire room held that same warmth and need to feel safe. A gentle breeze from an open window kissed his face.

"You are safe," an older woman said.

That voice took him out of his trance of bliss to panic once more. The cool breeze kissed the bare skin on his chest, and he looked around for that voice. One he did not recognize.

"There is no need—"

"What did you do to me?" Kace snapped, unable to form a proper thought.

She wasn't fazed by his outburst.

"You were dug out of the hospital collapse in the Hellion city. Your body was in grave condition."

None of this was making any sense. "What?"

"Arrangements were made in case the city was attacked

and you were unable to protect yourself. You have nothing to worry about," she explained.

Kace finally found the face to the voice. The woman was frail, but her body was only a vessel. Her eyes held wisdom and they locked onto Kace, not looking away in fear. There was no emotion. She had an intense gaze that made him unable to look away.

"You—"

"My sister?" he asked.

His voice was low. Kace was able to assess the situation enough to know he was in no position to make demands. But the flashes of memory of moments before the explosion caused his body to have a need to jump up and find her. Where was Nova?

"She is safe. You, Kace, are safe . . ."

He shook his head, wanting to know more, but the woman spoke before he had the chance to make a request.

"I know who you are: Kace, the bringer of pain and death. Your reputation is infamous, and with how you were able to calm yourself down means you're finally aware of the situation you find yourself in. You are smart, too smart for a child, but I do wonder why Eddison would risk everything to save the two of you."

Kace moved then. The woman held a power, one he could feel, but with the mention of his father's name, he moved. He didn't have the knowledge to defend his sister until he could understand his surroundings, but his father, he was taken. That white feather, he remembered. That Angel had him.

While she didn't scold him for standing, the first step he took away from the bed ended up with Kace on the floor. He tripped over something attached to his back, something long enough to create a pull that made his momentum uneven.

"Let me tell you a story, young one. A story you need to understand before you make your next move," she began, and Kace slowly turned his head to look behind him.

"Over two hundred years ago, a child was born. A child of fire, with hair as bright as a flame and soul of the purest form. That child was the only child of our coven elder, one who never shared the true origins of that child. It isn't the hair of fire or Wiccan blood that makes you connected, but the seal on your and your sister's back. It is one that child held since infancy."

Kace shook his head, trying to understand what he was hearing. The old woman's voice continued, regardless of whether he was listening.

"That boy showed strength not only in magic but in his ability to calm all of those around him. It wasn't his presence that created the warmth and comfort, it was his voice. Speculations and rumors surrounded this child's origins. It got to the point that his mother had no choice but to cast him out in fear of an uprising.

"He should have withered away and died, but he flourished in a world that worked against him. Never did he let the anger take control, everyone respected him—"

"I need to leave . . .," Kace whispered.

"You need to listen to me," she muttered and continued her story.

"Never once did he hold a grudge against his people for casting him out. But, on his mother's death bed, she told him who his father was, a secret that he still carries to this day."

Kace couldn't take his eyes from the wings behind him, and the voice he tried to use was no louder than a whisper when he spoke. "I can't do this . . ."

She continued, not listening to Kace's plea. "This coven may not openly admit it, but that boy was our protector. Because we are one of the last Wiccan clans, no one dares to challenge us because it will challenge him.

"You can identify a Wiccan by their purple eyes, but no one had hair like his, an unnatural fire, until you and your sister. The reason Eddison wanted us to protect you is because you are his children, aren't you?"

Nova's scream broke him out of his trance. Regardless of what he saw on his back, he had to get to Nova. The loud scream continued but those wings on his back—black wings—caught in the doorway. It caused Kace to fall backwards.

Curses spilled from his mouth before he found a way to tuck them in. His body reacted before his mind could comprehend, but when he saw his sister, he frowned. She had wings like he did that were moving uncontrollably. Wings of darkness, larger than their bodies. Tears streamed down Nova's face as her eyes started to glow yellow, and panic found Kace all over again.

"Nova. Hey sis, it's me," Kace said.

Everyone in the room was trying to calm the frantic woman. In these past few minutes, Kace learned more about his father than he had his entire life. There was nothing he could do to grasp this new information because if she got out of control, *they* would come.

"Nova—"

"Get away from me!" she screamed.

The yellow glow of her eyes was a warning that Dragons used right before they erupted. With her marking, she had the power to summon a protector, her mate, and if the King of Dragons appeared, this coven would be destroyed.

He leaped forward and wrapped his arms tightly around her. She continued to scream, thrash, but Kace held on, knowing she would come to her senses.

"I know this is scary, Nova, I am scared too. But I am here, and I will not let anything happen to you."

It took her a moment, but he felt her arms slowly wrap around him. His wings, she felt his wings and they were soft. They were like hers, they had wings . . .

The elders watched in the distance, no one disturbed them. As siblings who shared the same face and wings as dark as night's embrace, they knew their lives would get more complicated. It took Nova a few hours to calm down, but when she fell asleep, Kace still held his sister close.

"The forest whispers of the mate of the Dragon king. Many speculate it was an Angelic being," the older woman stated, walking up to the siblings.

"I appreciate you saving us, but we cannot stay here," Kace muttered.

"Having Angelic wings not of white means you also have Hellion blood within you."

"I can't . . . handle this," Kace admitted.

She nodded, understanding that this was all new to him. "Your father . . . where is he?"

Kace's mind kept reviewing everything he had learned. He was overwhelmed, out of his element, and knew if he acted poorly, it could get his sister killed. But, if this coven was in fact his fathers, were they truly safe?

"Are we protected even if we are mixed blood?" he asked in a serious tone.

"Our coven has been involved in your family's lives since your father was born. You and your sister are forever welcomed."

Kace leaned down and kissed Nova's forehead. She was safe, that was all that mattered. Kace always made sure his actions never reflected on his father or sister. If she could stay here until she wakes, he could investigate his bloodline. There were too many unanswered questions,

79

but he was going to find those answers, even if it got him killed.

His father had a seal on his back, did that mean he had wings too? These were Angelic wings. But, thinking about the story, it meant his father had lived for hundreds of years. Mortals did not live that long. Eddison never lied to his children, but they never asked the right questions. Those secrets stopped here.

*

Nova slept for a week. She heard voices around her, but when she opened those purple eyes, rather than her brother being at her side, she was alone. Reaching out, she touched the black feathers of her soft wings and smiled.

She had wings, like her husband's people. Nova hated being different from the Dragons, and these wings brought her closer to them. That smile did not fade, even when someone addressed her after realizing she finally was awake.

"Miss?" a woman called out.

It was a familiar older woman that appeared in the room that caused Nova to lose that smile. "I am glad to see you are awake."

Her eyes found that woman and Nova didn't feel threatened. When the woman asked her to follow, Nova slowly stood, showing no indication she was frightened. It was all because of the wings that rested gently on her back.

They felt natural, and she made them move as if they were another limb. After getting cleaned up, Nova dressed in a red dress that covered her body but left the mark of the

Dragons revealed. Her hair was wild, always untamed, and it caught everyone's attention. They seemed to know something she didn't, but Nova was more accepting of situations she couldn't control than her brother.

"Is that my father?" Nova asked.

The older woman stopped walking and looked at a painting of a mother and child. It was old but well maintained. There was no mistaking the red hair the child possessed, hair identical to her own.

"Your body and consciousness can separate. It took me and the others a lot of power to keep you from listening around the coven" was all she said.

Nova was always listening to the world around her. She called them dreams as a child, but when she got older, her father explained how she could hear but not yet see what was beyond the walls of the room she was in. She never chose to explore that fact but knew that what she remembered in her dreams were not always images she created.

"You know of me, elder, but I know nothing of you," Nova stated.

The woman nodded. "Indeed."

"My father trusted you, so I would like to extend that same trust, but—"

The older woman didn't let her finish that sentence. "Your brother uses his mind as a shield, and his body to show strength. You rely solely on what you—"

Everyone always looked down on Nova because she was a woman. Even though she shared the same face as her brother, everyone seemed to forget she had the same strength and, in some areas, she was stronger.

"Where is Kace?" Nova demanded.

Rather than wait for a response, Nova walked away. These people, she didn't know them, but they took her in. Her wounds had healed from the attack at the hospital, and with the arrangement her father made, Kace should be here too. She could always feel when he was around. There was no real reason behind that feeling, but she felt empty. He would never leave her alone; she refused to believe she was alone.

"Kace!" she shouted.

Symbols danced from her fingertips and scanned every building. This was her power. It was ancient and only became stronger with the bond from the Dragon king. She could see every building and feel every person as her eyes glowed a golden hue. Anger bubbled to the surface, but when she opened the door, rather than see her husband, all she saw was darkness . . .

IX

The darkness consumed her and forced her to once again sleep. Nova couldn't feel the world around her, couldn't sense the change, but when she heard her father's voice, that anger slowly melted away.

"Nova?" he whispered.

"Five more minutes . . .," she muttered and turned away from the sound of her father.

She forgot, only for a moment, that the world had changed. Her mind wanted to protect her and bring her right back to the comfort of her own bed, but when Nova got a mouth full of feathers, it came crashing down. Images of the building collapse, the coven, and Kace missing hit her hard.

She sat up and was now face-to-face with her father. He was alive and safe. Rather than be angry, tears slowly fell down her face. Nova adored her father and didn't want to believe that he left her. Eddison looked unharmed but his face was filled with worry. Never did her father show emotion. What was happening?

"She is ready for you," a new voice said.

It was the Angel. The one they saw only for a moment before the hospital collapsed. Nova's body tensed, but Eddison wrapped his arms around her to calm her down. He knew, as Kace did, what happened when Nova got angry.

"Give us a minute, Malcom," Eddison said.

The Angel, Malcom, rolled his eyes and walked out of the room.

"Father, what is going on? The hospital? The coven?" The questions spilled out of Nova's mouth the moment they were alone.

Eddison frowned at his daughter's confusion. Nova looked up to him, he knew that, but seeing those black wings on her back brought back a painful memory he was trying to hide from his children. But she deserved the truth. One he had no idea how to tell her . . .

"Listen to me," he began. "All that matters is that you and your brother are safe. This world, my daughter, is at war, one that you and Kace are not meant to be a part of. Those wings, they need—"

"I have wings!" Nova yelled.

"Nova—"

"Wings! I have wings and you hid them from me. I am part Angel, and by your expression, you knew I had wings!"

Everything was falling apart. That comfort of her home, her bed, was gone. Nova couldn't look at her father: he did this, he hid these wings from her. When she walked away, Eddison went to follow, but a wave of air from her wings pushed him back.

Nova had black wings. To have wings of feathers could mean anything, but the way they were presented and rested on her back meant Angelic blood was in her veins. Never would Angels hold something of darkness, which meant Hellion blood was also in the mix.

"Get out of my way!" she yelled.

Angels with golden armor appeared in front of her. She didn't know who she was or who her father could be. When her eyes glowed that familiar golden color, Dragon symbols appeared on the walls and floor, holding the soldiers in place. Every hallway she walked down, more and more Angels appeared.

She saw red. Her father kept a secret, a literal part of her dormant since birth. For Nova's entire life she felt different, an outcast, and this was why. She had no idea who she was supposed to be. The sense of Angelic presence continued to grow; she was no longer in the Mortal realm, but she did not care. Her brother left her, and her father lied. She had no one.

"Nova!" Eddison called in the distance.

When Nova turned a corner, a woman was standing there. She did not slow down. Raising her hands, a wave of wind from her wings pushed towards the woman, but her golden feathers blocked it. That woman's hair was as white as snow and was held back with golden clips and jewels.

The moment Nova approached, that woman turned her body to avoid a punch. Wrapping her arms around Nova with ease, she held the irate woman close to her.

"I know you are angry with your father and are scared," she began.

Nova struggled to get out of her grasp, but she continued to speak.

"You have every right to feel this way, but I will not allow you to harm others during your outburst."

Her voice sent a wave of calm through Nova, but those black wings went from soft to razor sharp instantly. The woman felt the sting of the feathers but refused to let her go. Nova continued to thrash and the building shook to reveal someone else had joined the situation.

"You need to let her go," Eddison demanded.

The woman's eyes slowly went from the screaming woman in her arms to Eddison. They both had red hair, a distinctive trait of an extinct race that only a few knew about. Nova had purple eyes like her father, but the shape, jeweled irises, and the wings of darkness belonged to the other part that created this child.

"Why are the Dragons here?" Malcom demanded, but Eddison held up his hands to plead with the woman.

"Please, Your Majesty—"

"I will never let her go . . .," the woman whispered, but she slowly opened her arms so Nova could escape.

Golden blood dripped from the woman's shallow cuts; ones created by Nova's black wings. It dripped onto her long white dress. She looked perplexed, but not entirely confused.

Nova could not stop running. Tears covered her vision as those wings tore apart everything they touched. She could hear him; a deep roar shook the entire building. To the untrained ears, all the Dragons sounded the same, but not to Nova. Each Dragon had a voice, and that voice belonged to one man.

She forced open the doors and the sky was filled with Dragons. They circled the building, surrounding it, ready to attack. Nova was not scared. She continued to run to one Dragon, the largest one waiting for her at the bottom of the stairs.

His scales glistened a golden shade and all his attention was focused on the woman with black wings. When Nova tripped, she did not fall because the Dragon was now a man, one that held his wife close as she cried out all the pain she currently felt.

Her wings cut Navar's hand as he held her close. There was no anger or shock in his expression, but there was worry. His eyes went from the wings to the woman with white hair and golden blood. Eddison was nearby, out of breath and panicking.

"I got you," Navar whispered.

The wings went soft as Nova wrapped her body around him. "I'm scared."

"Let's get you back home," he whispered, referring to his home, the one where she should have been all this time.

"Your Majesty," the woman in white called out.

Hearing the woman's voice caused Nova to cling to Navar harder. He picked up on that and looked up to that woman. "You and I have had no quarrel until today."

She only nodded, acknowledging that they needed to talk. Rather than take Nova far away, Navar brought her back into the place she woke up in. Nova was confused, as was Eddison, but Navar never let Nova go. Even when they sat down, his presence calmed her greatly, enough to listen.

"You bound her wings?" the woman in white yelled to Eddison after a long moment of silence.

"I am not your subject, nor is my daughter—"

That woman raised a hand to silence Eddison. "She holds the wings of Angels stained with the blood of Hellions. Where is her mother?"

Eddison went to approach, to defend his child, but Malcom prevented him from proceeding. There were too many secrets that revolved around Nova, and in her husband's arms she felt safe. The woman needed to think, needed to process what she learned.

"I want both of you out, now!" the woman in white demanded.

Eddison was not happy with that response. "You cannot command me. I will not leave my daughter!"

Nova looked at her father as he fought to stay with her. The Angel, Malcom, tried to help the guards, who appeared to take him out of the room. Eddison was showing emotion for the first time—raw anger, and fear. It wasn't till Eddison was taken out that the room quieted down, and silence filled the space.

"Separating a parent from their child is unlike you," Navar stated softly.

"Don't speak words you do not understand!" the woman snapped.

Navar kept a calm face. "I have known my wife since she was a small child. If I had known the bind was for wings, I would have brought her to you."

The woman continued to pace. Nova watched her, trying to read her body language. Agitation, anger, and anguish. It made no sense, but it was Nova who decided now was the perfect time to ask the right questions.

"Are you a princess?" she whispered.

The woman's expression softened with Nova's question. Slowly, she walked over to her and knelt. Everyone was calm, even Navar wasn't worried when this woman approached, which made Nova curious over fearful.

"No, my dear. I am the King of the Heavens."

When the king reached out and touched her face, it was warm and gentle. Never did anyone see the king so calm and open. With her other hand, she kept moving the loose strands out of Nova's face, trying to see her.

"You are so beautiful . . .," the king whispered.

"Mora," Navar warned.

"Why was I brought here?" Nova asked.

The king, Mora, ignored Navar's warning and focused solely on Nova.

"What is your name, young one?" she asked calmly.

"Nova . . ."

The king only smiled at the honesty Nova had produced. She stood, making sure to keep her movements where Nova could see them, and walked carefully away from the couple.

"Your guards can stay but your army needs to go. This is a guest house, you are welcome to stay if you stay out of my way," she said and walked out of the room.

Mora's entire demeanor changed. Nova looked up to her husband, confused, worried about it being something she had said. He could sense the tension in the room and outside these walls. Navar's mind was reeling with the knowledge that his wife, his chosen mate, was more than she appeared. He chose her not only for her ability to summon his kind and create a portal, but also because he loved her. A rare emotion for his kind to ever feel.

"Navar?" Nova asked, following his gaze out the nearby window.

"Your father broke Heavenly law by binding your wings. Am I to assume Kace has them as well?"

"No . . .," she replied, playing with the golden tassels on his suit.

"No?" Navar challenged.

"I need to find Kace."

Navar frowned. "You never cry, get scared, or cower in fear. For all three to happen at once shows me you are currently fragile. You learned a secret about yourself that he had no right in hiding—"

Nova stood and took a few steps away from him. "My father claims no allegiance to Hell or Heaven. He is neutral and that is what I want to be. I need to find my brother."

"You use my magic to fuel your spells. You are mine, Nova, regardless of formalities or title. Kace can take care of himself. I need you to stay with me. Please do not shut me out."

Nova only gave her husband a mischievous grin before walking out of the room. Navar sighed, following like she knew he would. Nova hid her pain and fear behind a smile and playful attitude. With each twirl of her dress, her eyes looked at the paintings on the walls. It was a world she had never seen before, but when she walked out onto a balcony, her eyes looked at the Angels flying through the sky.

"Is that what it is like? So open . . . and free?"

Navar went to her side and wrapped his arms around the woman he loved with all his heart. "I will have my soldiers look for Kace, but I want you to stay here and learn more about your wings."

"Will you stay with me? I do not want to be alone."

Navar smiled at his wife and kissed her lips gently. He would protect her, no matter what she chose to do. Those wings were her freedom from a world in which she didn't feel like she belonged. Now all he had to do was find that idiot brother who kept getting himself into trouble.

X

"Is that the best you got?" Kace spat.

His eyes were swollen shut and blood seeped from his mouth. A secret, a truth led him here, strapped to a chair and beaten. He couldn't drag Nova into this, her hands were clean, but his were stained.

Kace worked in the darkness; he knew what it meant to have wings of black. Only one Hellion race had wings with feathers covered in darkness. A breed that existed that everyone feared, and if they muttered the name, it would summon the nightmare.

"How am I supposed to talk to him if I cannot see him?" Kace yelled.

A bag was placed on his head once more: his captives were sick of looking at him. This was a camp led by one of the generals. Hellion's brilliant creations could never be tracked yet those they commanded were vast. Those generals were feared by mortals, Angels, and Hellions, but one was always close to the city. It piqued his interest.

"You've been rotting for four days, yet he still wants to talk to you. They tell me you can still see through those swollen eyes."

The voice gave him what he wanted: picked up once more and thrown into yet another cell. The bag was ripped violently off his head, and the first thing he could see through the swollen lids was *him*.

The man's face was covered, a mask with a blindfold holding the seal of the Hellion king. But it was his hair, white as the winter moon, that gave Kace relief. He found the right individual. The generals have similar features: white hair, black wings, and an underlying loyalty to their king like no one had ever seen.

"The Hellion city enforcer, the bringer of pain and death has been hunting me, why?" he signed with Kace silent.

His eyes were so swollen no one could see Kace's eyes. If they did, his Wiccan blood would have been known. They hunt his blood for its power, but the general could see in his own way, which made Kace show the utmost respect.

"You've been circling the Hellion city, following the Wiccan doctor, why?" Kace signed in return the moment his hands were freed.

His wings were bound to his back. Their freeing his hands was a gesture Kace would not abuse. He didn't respond quick enough, though, and the general appeared before him and pinned him hard to the ground.

In Hell, seven individuals were created for the sole purpose of destruction. No one knew their origins, their blood, but their strength was above all else. Kace was never afraid. All the stories of the seven generals caused him to hope for an impossible truth.

Kace couldn't move his body. The general focused on his wings. Drawing a blade, the Kace's wings turned razor sharp and went to attack. The general let him go and took a few steps back.

Those wings were a separate entity, yet a part of him. Rather than strike in retaliation, the general looked towards the red hair on his head. The unnatural color was too rare to be anyone else's. He had to be that Witch's son, and that meant everyone was about to be in trouble. The general gave Kace no warning. He kicked him hard in the head, rendering him unconscious.

*

The general's camp was temporary; they all move to avoid detection. Four generals were in the Mortal world at any point in time. The other three were to remain in Hell to protect their king. Their mission was to win this war, and this general had the knowledge to piece all the information he learned into a conclusion.

"Where is Dinah?" General Vadim signed, though he knew where she was.

He faced a wall of green flame in the comfort of his own quarters. The general was tall, built like a warrior, but his body language showed irritation. Within the flame were images of individuals that held similar qualities to what he possessed. Black wings with a blindfold holding the king's symbol.

"In rotation," one of the men signed. Which meant she was in Hell.

"Is something wrong?" another one asked with sign language.

There wasn't enough time to know who he could and could not trust. Evidence was gathered, but it was all through the word of a red-haired boy. This general had a job to do, and he didn't know if he should fully trust those he had fought alongside yet.

"No." He responded too quickly to ease the suspicion of those looking in through the flame.

"You wouldn't have contacted us if everything was fine. Why do you want Dinah?" one asked.

The general didn't hesitate in diverting the subject. He needed to think about how to approach this situation without fallout.

"Doesn't matter. I am taking on a ward. Make sure you inform the others."

"A ward?"

They all used sign language to communicate. With the face mask and barrier, their voices were taken to show obedience.

"The great Vadim who deemed no one is needed to ensure his victory is taking on a ward. What has changed?"

The general known as Vadim scoffed, raising his hands to respond. "Mind your business, Everard. Dinah has information that I seek. If you see her before I do, make sure you divert her to my camp. Till then, behave."

With a wave of his hand, the giant wall of hellfire vanished, severing the communication. A ward. A pupil that every general could have, to teach and mold into the perfect servant. Over the years, many soldiers trained under them, but no one had the opportunity to hold the title of ward.

Vadim knew the news would spread of the black-winged boy he took to train. Rumors would speculate on who he belonged to, but if he was Dinah's child, Vadim needed to protect him. Vadim remembered how calm Dinah was when he found her in her home. She got rescued by a Wiccan doctor and claimed him. He suspected she would procreate. Regardless of the reasons, she wasn't here to protect this boy, but Vadim was.

*

"You have been selected by General Vadim of His Majesty, the King of Hell's army. No questions. No comments. You will follow the routine and training of the army and report directly to the general. He gave me specific instructions to have you always wear the headdress and face protector."

Soldier. Kace was dragged out of that cell and thrown into a dry room. They no longer treated him like a prisoner but like a soldier. The general saw something when he saw his wings, and what was being asked of Kace showed that his suspicions of whose blood he shared were accurate.

He never wanted to be part of an army, Kace wanted control of his life, but this was the only way to get the answers he sought. His father had hidden everything that would have helped Kace feel whole.

The red hair that rested on top of his head needed to be covered, and the face mask he held in his hand bore the symbol of the Hellion king. A brand means that Kace chose a side. The one thing his father taught his children never to do.

Cleaned up and with his back to the soldier who came to check on him, Kace slowly put the mask on his face.

"Do you know sign language?" the soldier asked.

Kace did not respond. His built suggested strength, and when the soldier realized that he held black wings, he backed away. Fear. Because his wings held a certain build and color, fear was incorporated. Walking out into the camp, Kace held no regrets because this was the only way he would finally find his mother.

XI

Ten Years Later

"The Hellion forces have destroyed all remaining Mortal cities, and their support for our cause has plummeted. By doing nothing, we are losing this war!"

In a room in the Heavens, thirty people sat around a circular table. Some were graced with Angelic wings, while some had different variations to show their immortality. Thirty individuals to represent the current allied realms of Heaven.

"The Human realm is the bridge between the worlds."

Another interrupted. "But the mortals themselves are not needed to win."

"With the loss of territory, our troops are limited to where they can move."

"We need to discuss the generals."

That single phrase caused the entire room to fall silent and look to Navar, the King of the Dragons. His soldiers ruled the sky while the Angels protected the ground. It was a compromise, one made for a single purpose. Their silence caused Navar to growl.

"If we have to go through this every time, I will stop coming."

One responded, "Your wife and children hold similar qualities to the Hellion generals. Forgive us for doubting her loyalty, but an Angel cannot mate with a Hellion—"

Navar slowly stood but his gaze was piercing. "My family is off limits. You all have been previously warned what would happen if this subject came up again. Enjoy fighting this war without my aid."

"King Navar!"

He did not stop. These meetings were nothing he wanted to attend, but it was part of the treaty. A call to aid by the King of Heaven. It was no secret that a woman existed in the Heavenly realms with hair of fire and wings of darkness. People feared her instantly based on her description.

Nova had to work for years to gain people's trust, but one thing was always constant. Fear. Navar could protect her from the outside, but he couldn't separate her from the close friendship she'd formed with his king, one that he didn't fully trust.

*

"Haven't you grown into a nice, strong young man. Can't believe you are six months old already," Mora said playfully to the infant in her arms.

That boy wiggled playfully. His eyes were golden like his father's, and his hair was brilliant like the golden sun. This small child was strong both in body and spirit. A child fit to rule his father's kingdom.

As the infant continued to wiggle, his dark wings became loose from the swaddle he was in. His wings were a brilliant shade of midnight. Being a Dragon, he held no scales in his Human form, but if he fully transformed, the color could reflect the bloodline responsible for his wings. It was a proven fact, since his older brother had black scales versus golden.

"Your Majesty, Dr. Eddison is requesting an audience," a guard called out.

Mora frowned. The man who had a child of mixed blood could not leave her realm; she forbade it. All her actions were to protect Nova and her sons. Her reasons for such an action were never revealed, but when Eddison's daughter came to her kingdom for training and to visit, Eddison always seemed to find out.

"Toer dear, can you go and greet your grandfather," Mora asked the four-year-old boy who was reading a book nearby.

He had the same features as his infant brother. Golden hair and eyes, with black-feathered wings tucked gently behind his back. That boy was curious but obedient. Every month since Nova discovered her wings, she came with her husband to the Grand Assembly of Kings. That assembly lasted four days, and during that time, Mora watched Nova and her boys grow.

Nova trained with the royal guard and Mora's soldiers. She was determined to be strong. When her children came into the world, Mora dismissed herself from the meetings and spent time with those she held close.

"That bad?" Mora asked Navar.

The man appeared on a balcony. Mora used to hate that Navar had a way of sneaking up on her, but with his infant son in her arms, she knew she did not need to fear. Navar was watching her closely, as if expecting her to cause harm to the infant that carried his blood.

"Until they stop talking about my family—"

Mora smirked. "Do not do anything rash, Navar. Your family will always be safe in my realms."

"You cannot—"

"I can promise such a fate of you and yours. You do not appreciate the question regarding your wife's origin, and I do not appreciate how you question my loyalty to her."

"I never said such a thing . . .," he growled.

"You do not need to speak words in order for me to know your intent."

There was something in Navar's eyes, a darkness that only grew every time he looked at Mora. It wasn't there before Nova got involved, but now, it seemed Navar almost resented his king and the relationship she shared with his wife.

"You treat Nova as if she is your own child—"

"No, Navar," Mora interrupted.

"Nova is not my child, but I will protect her as if she was. Now, Keva and I are going to go and watch mommy train. You can deal with her father . . ."

Mora turned her back to the Dragon king and spread her golden wings.

"You hate Eddison because he bound her wings. I understand that, but your anger runs deeper. There's a reason you want him close yet as far away as you can have him."

"He needs to be protected, but he is also a reminder of how I failed so long ago. When Toer wants to join us, let him fly. Your children are the only Dragons I will allow to spread their wings in my kingdom."

Navar watched the King of the Heavens fly away holding his youngest son. She was not known to be kind or fair, so how she treated his family bothered him. There was little he could do without risking war, but he would do whatever it took to keep his family safe. Even if it was from a woman who claimed to want what was best for them.

*

Anger. Every day when Nova looked into the mirror, she saw her brother. He left her at the coven, alone and confused. How dare he leave her. Ten years. That was how long it had been since she had seen him, and the fear for his safety had turned to anger.

A sword was her weapon of choice. Even though her wings were as sharp as blades, she used them as a shield like Mora taught her. Nova had so many questions that would never be answered, but the holy blade given to her by Mora was the power she needed to feel strong. She trained for ten years to be able to carry such a weapon, and if she wasn't already the Dragon queen, she would be ruling armies with how quickly she became fluent in battle.

"It is becoming unfair to my generals to have you continue to train with their soldiers. If they are chosen to fight, none of them will be conscious enough to go."

Mora landed next to a woman who stood in the circle of unconscious Angels. The landing was silent, but the woman turned her body to see Mora and the child she held. A child that seemed aware of who was before him.

"Did he withdraw his army?" Nova asked, but rather than speak, she used her hands to ask the question.

To wield a holy weapon and harness its strength, a vow needed to be made. It could be anything a person is willing to give, and with Nova, she took a vow of silence. No words had been spoken since she started to train. With her hair braided tightly against her head and dressed in the armor of her husband's people, she was ready to fight.

"It seems you are still a topic of conversation."

The child in Mora's arms reached actively for his mother. He nor his brother feared the sight of blood, death, or pain that war could bring. Taking a few steps forward, Nova took her son into her arms, but not even his warmth could ease the anger that existed on her face.

"You know I do not approve of your need for violence, but I will not have you unprepared in case you need to fight," Mora began, but Nova was focused solely on her son.

"What drives you, Nova?" Mora added, but like always, she did not get an answer.

During these past ten years, Nova had never answered that question. Even though the trust had been established, secrets still existed. Mora was patient, but that patience was wearing thin when it came to the risk of her losing Nova.

*

"Father!" Toer called out.

Navar stayed on the balcony, knowing his family would return to him. Never did they stay apart too long. When he turned to look at his firstborn, Eddison was right behind him. Both men had an agreement, one that ensured Nova and her children would be protected, even if Eddison was separated from them. The man could not go into the Dragon realm and came to the realization he was now captive in the Heaven king's world. But four days a month, Navar brought his family, and Eddison could have some light in his dark future.

"Why don't you get the drawing you made for your grandfather? I bet he would love to see it," Navar said to Toer, who ran off while his grandfather approached.

"You wanted to speak with me?" Eddison asked in a monotone.

Navar nodded. "Ever since Toer was born, Nova has been teaching him magic. Within the books she has, not one of them speaks of portals."

Eddison gave a slight shrug. "There are many different types of magic."

"Yet none of them I can find speak of portals. I do not know about the Wiccan practice, but in all the books Nova has in our realm, it doesn't explain the strength she has in

103

being the key to the Dragons. One race can produce the portals, and they are not Mortal."

Eddison was silent. He never gave any indication to any inquiry about his people. Mora and Navar had asked many times, but each time, he chose to stay silent. It was the only way to protect his family, even if it meant he would never see them again.

"Nova told me what she learned from your coven all those years ago. The story of a man born of an elder whose father was unknown. He also has a longer than average life span and can do great things with little effort. I do not want lies, Eddison. My family is involved—"

"I have never lied to you," Eddison responded in a whisper.

"Then you can answer this question for me, and I want the truth. Are you a gatekeeper?"

Eddison never lied. But answering Navar's question would take careful thought. Leaning up against the railing, he looked away from the Dragon king.

"Did you mark my daughter because she was the key to your realm?" Eddison asked.

"Yes," Navar responded, not hesitating, but he continued to speak rather than let Eddison answer the previous question.

"We can sense our gatekeepers, the ones chosen for our realm. That seal wasn't to hide her wings, but her connection to me. Make no mistake, Eddison, I love your daughter now that she is grown but that love came later."

"Ask your question . . .," Eddison mumbled, getting irritated.

"There can only be one gatekeeper per realm, but they were thought to be destroyed many years ago. But, if this is truly what I think it is, I know of three that are living. Are you, Eddison, the gatekeeper of the Heavens?"

"Yes," Eddison replied.

"Was your seal the coven spoke of to hide that fact?"

Eddison slowly nodded. "I removed my seal years ago when Mora figured it out. You seem to be slow in gathering all this intelligence."

Navar smirked. "I have a wife and children. What have you heard regarding Kace?"

Both men fell silent after the question was asked. Kace. Neither Eddison nor Nova had any knowledge of where he was or if he was still alive. Navar was true to his word: he kept searching for the missing twin with no results. The war was now at a tipping point, and Navar knew it was only a matter of time before his wife got involved.

XII

"My dear, I need you to wake up," a gentle voice whispered as those ruby lips kissed his shoulder.

Ten years. For ten long, agonizing years Kace had fought for the Hellion army. Pain refused to let him go. It changed him, made him cold and withdrawn from this world. He was crafted into what the King of Hell required, an obedient soldier.

"Kace," that voice repeated.

Those ruby lips slowly caressed his skin. A simple peck from his shoulder all the way to his back. Those lips were gentle, finding every piece of skin not covered by his black wings that rested against his back.

"My love . . ."

Peck. Each scar she found was kissed. Every mark was loved, and slowly the woman crawled on Kace's back, getting better access to the body in her bed. She was bare, the long dark hair covering her body as she continued to kiss him. Gentle touches. It was her, this woman, who fully gained Kace's trust, a gift he gave no other.

"I know you hear me . . .," she whispered and gently bit down.

A playful smile formed on Kace's face when the woman got there. She kissed his cheek, his jawline, and eventually his nose. His face was more rigid, with small scars finding their way to the surface. Kiss. But when she got to the blindfold, she frowned.

The blindfold was a mark, a declaration to his king. Kace did not have any markings in their bed—no soldier of the king would stain her sheets—but that blindfold he refused to take off. General Vadim had one and he was feared like Kace. The rumored eighth general was sleeping happily in her bed and not one ounce of fear crossed her mind.

A voice from across the room made the mood quickly fade away.

"Forgive my intrusion, Your Majesty. The council is waiting."

"Kace," the woman said less playfully, knowing that their time was coming to an end.

Kace's breathing never changed but the first moment she kissed him, he was awake. When the woman went to move from him, Kace reached up and pulled her into his embrace. He moved fast enough that it took her by surprise.

"Careful . . .," she said, a small laugh forming on those ruby lips.

His body was hard. Built for war. Which meant he wasn't a comfortable pillow, but she snuggled close to him, knowing times like these were few and far between.

"Be careful today. I do not trust the undead," Kace whispered into her hair.

She frowned. "I can handle myself."

"I have no doubt, but I still want you to request a mediator.

"Regardless of what—"

Kace did not let her speak another word. He found her lips and took what was his. They both were bare, a black silk sheet covered parts of their bodies, but the bracelet Kace wore, one that had the mark of the King of Fae, was one he wore proudly.

It was a claim. Within the Hellion race, a Hellion cannot claim another, but this was how she did it. A simple promise to always find their way back to each other, no matter the distance that grew between them.

"Did you want to try that sentence again?" Kace teased when he broke the kiss.

She smiled. "Are you trying to tell me what to do, gatekeeper?"

As quickly as Kace moved, she moved faster, pinning him down so she was once again on top. He didn't fight, only looked up at the most beautiful woman he had ever seen.

"I am," he teased.

She glared at the man below her. "You must—"

"I will not risk your safety."

That one sentence made all the tension in her body release. She knew he wanted to protect her, but being the King of the Fae, Layla refused to allow anyone to take control over her. Even if their intentions were pure.

"I do not need your protection, Kace, but never forget that you are mine. Regardless of your king's mark resting on your face, I own you."

Kace smirked. "You can use me all you want."

"If you wanted to watch over me, all you had to do was ask. But for now, I have some business to attend to that will sadly take me out of this bed."

He watched as she finally stood and walked towards her closet. The room wasn't vast, but it was big enough for the two of them to feel protected. No windows, only one door and an endless closet to hold everything they would ever need. This was his paradise, with the one woman no one would ever suspect of sharing his bed.

"Be safe," Layla whispered into the darkness, knowing that if she looked towards Kace, he would see the worry on her face.

When he would leave, he would go back to the battlefield. This was the only place she knew he was safe, and when she looked away, she knew that he may never come back . . .

XIII

When Kace wasn't with Layla, he was where Vadim required him to be. Heaven may have thirty realms in its alliance, but Hell had over one hundred. The promise of strength and wealth was the driving force of many Hellions, but their loyalty was only as far as their fear. A war existed on the Mortal plane, but the fight amongst the Hellions was far greater than anyone anticipated.

"The general requests your presence," a soldier announced through a tent flap.

Kace rocked back and forth, his body still humming from his morning with Layla. His attention was not to the soldier but to the monitors in front of him. His skin was hidden under the layers of clothing and metal armor they forced him to wear, but his face, that golden mask was the key in not only hiding his eyes but also his hair.

The soldier knew better than to get up from the kneeling position. It did not matter how long it took Kace to acknowledge him, he needed verification that the message was delivered. All Kace could think about was Layla, a woman he accidently stumbled upon when he found his way into her realm.

Gatekeeper. A word that no one knew. His attraction wasn't only physical because of the gatekeeper bond, but his need to protect and educate was why he quickly became obsessed with her. His woman knew who he was the moment she captured him, and for the last five years, he found his way into her bed, and she found a way into his heart.

"I will see the general," Kace said, allowing the soldier to leave.

Kace knew what was going to be said. It happened every time he snuck away. When he walked into the general's tent, he bowed out of respect, but his body language showed playfulness.

"I asked you to tell me when you visited her. Why did I find your bed empty this morning?" Vadim signed in irritation.

Vadim was his mentor, the only person that knew the truth of where his mother could be. A truth he had yet to share with him. Being the highest-ranking officer in this army, Kace couldn't demand the knowledge, but he respected the man and all that he taught him through the years.

"I know you want to know every time I have a bedding experience—"

Vadim raised his hand to silence Kace.

"She is using you. I have told you this. You are her gatekeeper, and she would have killed you if you didn't hold His Majesty's mark."

111

Kace could see through the mask and watched his mentor's hand form every word. They held sincerity and concern, but Kace shrugged.

"I accepted her claim and I carry her mark, but she knows my loyalty is always to my king. Did she contact you?"

Vadim reached down for a piece of paper on the table and held it up.

"Your idea I assume?" he signed.

Kace shrugged once more.

"If you were not good with your hands, I would have disposed of you years ago," Vadim finished.

Kace could not help but raise his hand to respond, knowing what he was about to say was for nobody but Vadim. "That is what I am always told."

The banter was light. Years of fighting side by side created trust, protectiveness, and openness to answer questions, which made Kace's life an open book for Vadim. But when an explosion occurred in the distance, all banter stopped. They did not communicate with each other; they moved out of their separate exits and summoned their soldiers.

*

War created a never-ending movement, one that could only end with the death of another. Peace was a story that everyone craved, but no one could write without blood. Every sword strike or fist that flew caused a life to end. Kace felt every death and finding himself standing on top of a pile of bodies, his attention was to the blood dripping from his hands.

"A need for aid has been approved, but General Vadim says you are to report to the King of Fae for the meeting of the undead," a soldier reported.

Kace let out a heavy sigh. This fight was a slaughter. Mortals were trying to protect themselves and regain control of their lands. They stood no chance and fought bravely. He did this all in the name of the king, the one who he hated with his entire being.

*

Layla was patient but not forgiving of tardiness. This meeting was not set up by her, but she agreed to attend if she had a mediator from the king. It wasn't that she didn't trust in her ability to destroy the undead if they did something unkind, but she wanted Kace at her side if she could.

"Thank you, King Layla, for coming all this way," a man with decaying flesh announced.

The smell was horrid, but Layla kept a straight face. These creatures were mindless drones that were fighting for a say in their own lives, a voice that the king would never allow. The Fae were magical beings that used the energy of the world around them to create movement. They too have been trying to gain respect from the king, and it was their fight that caused the curse to fall on their people, a curse that all men will die and never again be reborn.

"By calling me here, you are not only putting myself but also my people at risk," Layla spoke.

The man bowed slightly. "Like I, you have been cursed by the king. Your women need to fight rather than grow and raise a family. You rely on claims to make sure your race doesn't go extinct, so you soil your bloodlines. I think it is wise to hear what I have to say."

"I will not openly defy the King of Hell," Layla proclaimed.

The man laughed. "Dear Layla, so beautiful yet naïve. Your mother—"

"She agreed to stand up against him and burned for it. I will not have that fate fall on my people!"

"She fought for what was right! You are more of a mindless creature than I will ever be. If you will not side with me, then I have no more use for you!" the man screamed.

"I may not agree with the king, and my reasons to despise him are my own," Layla sneered.

The man took a step towards her. This meeting took place in an abandoned cave outside the man's realm. It was protected and vacant from all ears of the king. It was also a tomb in his mind if Layla failed to comply.

"Your women are no match for the armies of the generals. I will enjoy taking your place when you burn."

Layla watched him take another step closer. The man believed he had the upper hand, but she laughed. That laughter brought confusion, and Layla raised her hand to announce another visitor.

"Because we are women does not mean we are weak. I have alliances, an army, a general of my own. So, my fears do not compare to the threats you brought before me."

Bodies with decaying flesh surrounded her. She appeared to be alone, her soldiers were asked to wait outside, and she agreed. But, when Kace's soldiers filled the room, the man looked towards Layla, mortified. It was then he saw Kace standing behind her, dripping with the blood of his freshest kill.

"Do you mean to tell me that you tamed this beast? The rising eighth general!"

The shock was obvious on the creature's face, but Kace stood firm. His attention was forward, waiting for permission from his woman to attack.

"They are monsters controlled by the Hellion king. If you side with him, you damn everyone. This was all a trap . . . attack!"

With a nod from Layla, Kace raised his hand. That signaled his soldiers to take a step forward. The decaying soldiers that littered the space continued to run forward, and when they got close, Kace lowered his hand, signaling the attack.

When the forces collided, the noise echoed off the cave walls. Ripping flesh and gurgling screams were something Kace was used to, but when he walked in front of Layla, he made sure she was focusing on him.

"You do not need to be here," Kace whispered.

She didn't say anything. Layla was the King of the Fae, she needed to be strong, and when objects came flying towards her, Kace raised his wings. They were a shield, allowing all that would cause her harm to bounce off him. He held her protectively, knowing no one could see her vulnerability.

"Aren't you glad you listened to me?" Kace teased, knowing she needed to get out of her own thoughts to realize what was happening around her.

Layla blinked and looked up to the man she loved. Raising a hand, she saw blood from where she held onto his arms. That sight made her frown.

"You're wounded."

Kace smirked. "Is that worry I hear in your voice?"

Layla growled but noticed that her dress was stained with blood. It wasn't the blood of the ones he killed: cuts were all over his body and blood seeped out open areas of his armor.

"Where else are you injured?"

"I am fine—"

Layla knew he was lying to her. His body wasn't as balanced as it normally was, but the hold he had on her was strong. She took a deep breath and looked back towards his face, wanting to see those eyes but knowing that fight was for another time.

"Watch yourself, gatekeeper, you carry my seal, and I can order you to your death if I feel the need."

"Get in line, love," Kace whispered in a chuckle.

The hold he had on her loosened and Kace fell forward. He was too large for Layla to carry, so she fell along with him. The fight was over by the time Kace fell unconscious to the ground, and Vadim was now looking down at the two. Layla didn't know the general followed Kace, but when he moved his hands to communicate, she followed the words with ease.

"You are young, but I have respect for you and your people. By claiming this boy, he gave you an army that wasn't his to hand over."

"You do not command me," Layla growled.

"I will honor his vow of protection, if you allow him to walk away if he so chooses."

Layla felt the blood starting to pool around her. Kace needed medical attention, and she was not in the position to help him. Bodies littered the ground around them (it was an easy victory for the soldiers of Hell), but Vadim waited for her response, even if it meant Kace would bleed to death.

"We will talk another time. Save him," she finally said.

Vadim reached forward and picked up Kace. The general was calculated in his movements. He never engaged without understanding all his options, but Kace was reckless and emotional. That emotion started to show within Vadim, and his change of actions was noticed by all those around him.

XIV

Hell was not all brimstone and pain. It had a beauty reflected in its blackened sea and endless night. It was a calming sight that the king overlooked from his castle, trying to find the answers to his current problem.

The castle glistened with marble and steel. Its vibrant wealth showed the power the man who owned it held. A power that he inflicted with fear and pain. It didn't matter the reason, no one disobeyed him.

"The undead?" he asked.

His back was to a wall of hellfire, one that reflected the generals currently residing in the Mortal world. Those in the flame and the ones who were here in person bowed before their king. He was a man known as Nobu, one with long hair the color of ice and eyes that reflected the fire he possessed. He was a man that held all the pain in the world. Even his seven greatest creations that were meant to bring him victory failed him yet again.

"Don't make me ask again," Nobu growled.

"Destroyed," Vadim signed from within the flame.

"The Fae king?"

"Still loyal," Vadim responded.

Seven individuals were before him. They all had hair as pale as the moon and his symbol covering their eyes.

Perfect warriors that would not fail him, but when Nobu's eyes went to the only woman amongst them, he grew angry. There was so much hate in his eyes for her. That hate caused him to walk over and hit her hard across the face.

"Sirens?" he called out.

The two generals that were there in person did not come to her aid. They knew better than to interfere.

"Loyal," Vadim signed.

Nobu struck her once more before looking back to the flame.

"Good."

Vadim bowed and the flamed vanished, leaving only Nobu and the three generals before him. Looking away from *her,* he focused on the two that were still silent.

"I want the two of you to go to the Mortal realm and track the general that took on a ward. Learn all you can about him and his student. Report everything back to me," Nobu ordered.

The two generals slowly stood and bowed. They did not acknowledge the female general. Nobu waited until he was truly alone with her before picking her up by her hair and dragging her across the room. Rage. It was all directed towards her, but never once did she fight back.

For the past thirty years, the only female general, Dinah, had been chained to the castle. She had been beaten, tortured, and yet, she endured it without an ounce of rebellion. The king expected her to fight, but when she didn't, he knew she was hiding something.

"Tell me of their movements!" Nobu demanded.

His appearance meant a great deal to him. When he was done with Dinah, he cleaned his hands of the blood he spilled and focused on the task at hand. He didn't care if they had names or feelings, they were nothing more than a tool.

"The two you sent out will reach the Mortal world in two days," a servant reported.

"Good."

The servant looked towards its king.

"Who do you want recalled back?" they asked.

Nobu heard the question and ignored it. His mind was on a different topic that he needed answers to immediately.

"Tell me what you know of the ward," he demanded.

There was a large sphere that floated in the center of the room. It was his eyes, powered by the stars in the sky. Within that sphere, a picture formed of Kace standing on top of Mortal bodies. His uniform was stained with blood, and his golden mask was covered in the remains of his enemies. It was the black wings that always got the king's attention.

"Origin?" Nobu hollered.

"Confirmed Hellion and Angel hybrid. No suspected Heaven loyalties and has earned your mark by actions on the battlefield."

Nobu needed more.

"Why did he take a ward?"

The servant rushed to get the words out.

"It was an extension of his power. You assigned him to oversee a large population, and the ward has been helpful."

Nobu never looked away from the images. Kace's movements were precise, and he never hesitated to take down his enemy. The king was waiting for the one thing he needed to confirm his suspicion, but the moment Kace spread his wings, the connection severed.

There was something or someone preventing him from seeing. The king knew only a handful of people possessed that kind of power, and it seemed they wanted to protect this ward. Which made the suspicions that he wasn't who he claimed rise. Nobu would find the answers, even if he had to slaughter all his generals to do it.

XV

"Allowing him to pass freely between realms not only puts you in danger but Kace as well!"

Vadim was furious. Not only did the meeting with his king not go as planned, but he still had Layla and Kace to deal with. It was insane that the two took such risks to be together. Vadim didn't understand it, and no amount of warning seemed to change the couple's mind.

"What my gatekeeper does is none of your business, General. IF you released him from your command and gave him to me like I proposed, he wouldn't have to move between realms."

She was not leaving his camp, but at least Layla gave Vadim space to think. The Hellion armies acknowledged all forms of royalty in the Hellion alliance, but their true loyalty was always to the Hellion king.

Vadim walked out of the tent, furious with Layla's proposal. He was now face-to-face with three individuals he never expected to see together. Four generals in one place was a bad omen, and for them to be here without their armies showed it was personal and not ordered by the king.

"What do I owe the pleasure?" Vadim signed when he and the three generals were under the protection of his tent, away from prying eyes.

"The king is sending Reid and Qued to the Mortal world," Everard signed in a panic.

All four of them were identical in appearance. It wasn't only their clothing that made them identical, it was their body, face, and mannerisms. It was as if they were bred from the same hole they crawled out of, but people knew better than to whisper their suspicions out loud.

"Who is going back?" Vadim responded.

"No one," Kelby replied.

They all had the same mask and the same device that took away their ability to speak. They all were fluent in sign language, giving them the ability to communicate with each other. Even if they couldn't use their eyes to see, they always knew what was said.

"What purpose does he have with six of us in the Mortal world?" Vadim asked.

The moment his words left his fingertips, it all snapped into place. Dinah. She had been banned from leaving the castle for the last thirty years, and Reid and Qued coming here meant she would be alone with Nobu. Vadim moved without thinking, but the three generals grabbed him before he made it out of the room.

"You've never reacted on emotion or moved without calculating the risks," Hadwin signed, pushing Vadim back into the room.

"Ever since you took in that ward, you slowly started to act out of character," Kelby added, but it was Everard who demanded what they all were thinking.

"Show us your ward!"

Vadim was careful, always cautious, but it seemed he was slipping. The two people that were connected were now exposed to the world he was trying to protect them from. Vadim did everything he could for Kace, but without Dinah, there was only so much preparation before they all would be tested.

*

"I am always amazed at your ability to heal," Layla observed.

She sat on the bed, watching Kace limp around the room, trying to piece himself back together. Between Layla's magic and an unseen force, Kace was never down for long. His wounds to the flesh were healed enough not to reopen, but his movement showed fatigue was evident. He truly was a stubborn man.

"Be honest with me, Layla," Kace began but flinched when he moved the wrong way.

"When am I not?" she teased.

"Are you part of the rebellion against the king?"

Layla fell silent at the question as she watched Kace slowly button his pants. His familiarity with technology showed Layla he had been in the Mortal world for some time, but his comfort with her magic . . . all Hellions seemed to fear it. Between the Hellions' fear and the Angels not trusting her, she became curious as to what creatures bore this man.

His body should reject her magic, but his gatekeeper blood showed her that there was something more to the mangled love they shared. If she were to fully trust him, all his secrets needed to be revealed.

"What are you thinking about?" Kace asked, but Layla remained silent.

She stood and walked towards a table. It was behind the door and that door swung open quickly, hiding Layla by accident. Kace turned to look at the three generals before him and Vadim in the doorway. Out of custom, Kace immediately took a knee.

The first thing Everard, Kelby, and Qued saw was the black wings. The likeness to their own was undeniable. Hadwin took a step forward, but Vadim grabbed his arm to prevent him from getting any closer.

Kace's hair was revealed. That hair was a symbol that Vadim didn't tell him about, and Kelby was the first to acknowledge what was in front of them.

"You found a gatekeeper? Their race is extinct," he signed.

"Red hair could mean anything," Everard interjected, but Hadwin finished the thought.

"No Angel would willingly bed a Hellion. The purity of their blood cannot succumb to claim unless the Hellion is a royal. Who does he belong too?" he signed urgently.

None of the generals were innocent in their bedding practices. To have black wings—it was too much for Hadwin to process, but he looked to the others to try and find some guidance. With everyone so preoccupied with Kace, no one saw Layla creep out from behind the door.

"Are you insane?"

"There is nothing saying he is one of ours."

125

"What else could it be?"

"Fuck that! If anyone of us sired a child, we would feel it."

Kace watched as they bickered amongst themselves. Red hair equals a gatekeeper? If he was a gatekeeper, could that mean Nova was too? The Dragons. Kace realized what it meant to have Navar in Nova's life, but his mind couldn't prepare him for Hadwin picking him up and pinning him against the wall.

"I want answers!" Kelby demanded, signing towards Vadim.

Vadim kept his focus on Kace. Everyone wanted answers and they all were looking to him. Raising his hand slowly, the words he formed next shocked everyone for different reasons.

"He is Dinah's son."

Dinah. Kace knew there was only one female general but never her name. There were whispers of a Dinah in the Hellion city he grew up in, and they feared her like they did him. The shocked expression was on Kace's face when all four generals fell to the ground. But rather than being on the ground, Kace was pressed up against the wall.

"You and I had an agreement, Vadim," Layla stated, walking out from behind the door.

None of the generals could move, but they all could hear the king walking closer.

"If my gatekeeper is treated well, you can use him. But, by the look of the four Hellion generals teaming up against him, I say the agreement is no longer valid."

126

Layla could see that Kace was overwhelmed. She tried hard not to care about his feelings, but moments like this made it impossible. She reached out and touched Kace's shoulder, allowing both to disappear in an instant.

When Layla vanished, the generals could move. Vadim was the only one that didn't stand; he looked up to the three generals who demanded answers.

"He is the gatekeeper to the Fae?" Hadwin signed.

"Dinah had a child?" Kelby demanded to know.

Everard was the only one who didn't demand an answer but stated all he knew.

"Dinah had a child, and you knew. It was the reason why you petitioned the king to give her a year."

The other two didn't take note of what Everard noted, they kept demanding answers.

"You let her take him? He is your ward!" Hadwin signed.

Vadim raised both of his hands, demanding silence before he finally gave them something they wanted.

"When Kace comes back looking for answers, I will give them to him. Kace knew as little as we did when he approached me looking for his mother. Reid will kill him if he finds out and before Dinah can explain herself. We will keep him safe," Vadim signed and they finally all were silent.

XVI

It was not only the Hellions that were starting to revolt. The thirty realms in Heaven wanted to fight back, regain their territory, and live their lives. They wanted blood, and even though Mora said she wanted peace, she was an invading party with no end in sight.

"I want to be at the next assembly," Nova signed in front of her husband.

Navar was covered in mud and the elements. He had a routine that took him to all his outposts every morning. The king wanted to see for himself that his realm was secure. Rather than getting cleaned up, Nova cornered him in the hallway.

"We have already been over this, Nova," Navar said as his feisty Dragon queen put a finger on his lips.

He was upset when she gave up her voice for the holy weapon. He has not heard her laughter since before her children were born. But her fierceness, it was all in the eyes. Before any of them could respond, a soldier bowed.

"Your majesties, a messenger is in the war room," he reported.

"Who is calling?" Navar demanded.

"The Seers."

Seers are oracles that hold the ability to foresee the different layers of the past, present, and future. It was nothing more than a suggestion of what could happen, good or bad. Navar wanted to believe the future was in the hands of the individual, which was why he hated the Seers and their suggestions.

"Tell them to bother someone else," he growled.

Nova didn't make any remarks, she walked around her husband and towards the war room. Navar might not believe in magic, but his wife did.

The moment the two of them walked into the room, they felt cold.

The creatures were lifeless bodies floating a few inches off the ground. Possessed. Undead. It was a fine line between loyalty to their king and peace. They appear to offer a choice, but it was a wager Navar refused to believe.

"This is not for you, Dragon King. It is for your gatekeeper," one spoke, and Navar moved in front of Nova protectively.

"A voice was lost so a weapon could be gained, but the other half gave up his eyes for the truth he was not ready to hear. Eyes. Mouth. Two halves of a whole that chose not to listen."

The Seers were talking about Kace, the brother Nova yearned to find. This was not Nova's first time dealing with these beings, and she knew if she wanted more, it would come at a price.

"What do you want?" Navar demanded.

"Want is for those who seek comfort, we seek peace. Find the missing halves and all will turn in your favor, but

129

be warned, the darkness and light hold a secret no one can understand."

They came and went in an instant. Always dramatic, but when Nova blinked, she was no longer in the war room but stood on a pile of bodies. She could feel the blood dripping down her body as her heart beat uncontrollably.

"Your brother will rise and have an army that will be unstoppable. Which side he chooses will be the victor. Find him. Stop him. Hell cannot win."

The voice was clear, and Nova watched the destruction around her. Kace did this and the Seers feared him. They wanted him dead because he tipped the balance.

"Nova, dear . . . follow my voice . . ."

Mora's voice gently broke through the chaos that surrounded her. Kace felt so close. For the first time, Nova felt her brother and all she wanted to do was reach out for him, but when Nova took one step off the mountain of bodies, her body collapsed.

"What do you mean, possessed?" Navar demanded.

Nova could not move but she could hear the voices around her.

"The Seers tried to use her to summon someone, and because she is connected to me, I felt the pull. Why would they approach you and not me?" Mora yelled.

"Is she safe?" the Dragon king asked.

"She is now protected. What did they tell you?"

Navar frowned. "All texts on the gatekeepers were destroyed by the former King of Heavens and the current King of Hell. The myth that they are the power of the gods has bounced around, but the truth is never known. If the gatekeepers are being reborn, what don't I know?" Navar asked.

Mora looked towards Nova. "You and I found our gatekeepers by accident, and thankfully, they are weak enough so they can be trained. These creatures are known as the key and hold the power to destroy their chosen realm, which is why my husband feared them."

"If you knew this, why didn't you tell me?"

Mora closed her eyes to control her emotions. "Eddison and Nova are rebirths of a being that will disturb the balance. Their influence on their kings can destroy everything we built . . ."

"Tell me more?" Navar asked.

Mora didn't want to talk about it, but she knew that Navar wouldn't let this go.

"Why do you want to know something that doesn't—"

"This is my family you are talking about. My wife will react to what she went through, and if I can control that reaction, I can protect her from making a mistake . . ."

The noise faded. The next time Nova was able to open her eyes, it was to the loving face of her firstborn son.

"Mommy?" he asked. The fear was seen in those golden eyes.

That small boy had the whole world on his shoulders. He didn't even know the burden he was given by being born first. So small and fragile, but that boy was hers, and Nova would do whatever it took to protect him.

"Why are you so sad?" he asked.

All she could do was smile, bringing him close to try and ease that concern. Nova remembered when he came

into this world. Her husband was at her side with Mora. His cry was music to their ears, and the world got scarier when she held him for the first time.

Nova wanted to sing, to tell him everything was going to be alright, but she gave up that right to fight. War was a reality, and no one was immune to its horror. When that boy fell asleep, she slowly stood and tucked him in. The fear in her eyes wasn't for the battle that was to come but for the idea that she may never see him again.

The oracles showed her the truth and it replayed in her mind. They feared Kace for what he did and what he would do. Why would Kace go to the Hellions? Never once did he choose a side, but now, Nova felt that if she ever found her brother, she wouldn't recognize him.

XVII

"In the wake of the most recent destruction, a state of martial law has been declared. The following statement has been released: 'All Hellion and nonmortal cities are forbidden to approach. No one will be out of their home after dark . . .' "

The news reported what was transpiring. The endless fighting was taking its toll on everyone. Nova could feel the tension, the fear, as she walked the familiar streets. This was once her home, but nothing about it felt familiar.

That uneasy feeling was accompanied by guilt. After leaving her husband's realm, Navar would never forgive her. She gave no notification and used her magic to block her seal. He would not be able to find her.

"Get out of my way!"

"Move!"

Everyone was fighting to survive. There was no order. Nova pushed her way through the littered streets, knowing that if she needed to defend herself, she was more than capable. But standing in front of her home, the only one on the street still standing, she felt empty. It felt empty.

"I wouldn't go in there," a child whispered.

Nova looked down to the child covered in dirt and bruises. She didn't respond, but the child finished his thought.

"It is haunted . . ."

The child did not elaborate but that explained why her childhood home felt like it was frozen in time. Nothing was taken or destroyed. When Nova walked into the kitchen, it was as if they never left. She was happy, they were happy, but it was an illusion.

"You're late," a woman stated.

Nova jumped when she walked into her old room. She thought there wasn't another soul in this house, and to have this woman be here without her knowing raised her guard. That woman was lying on her back, relaxing on a bed that once was hers.

"I apologize for him . . ."

Nova didn't understand what that woman meant, but she felt a hand wrap around her from behind and cover her mouth. Her wings went to expand, but something wrapped around her back, encasing and immobilizing her wings.

"We need to make this quick."

She tried to move but the hands held her tightly. All the years of training made her body able to fight, but the weight they put on her wings drained all the energy she had. Fight. She needed to fight.

"The less you struggle, the less force we will have to use."

That woman was in charge. Nova struggled, tried to kick, to hit, but whoever held her was stronger. She was not weak; she refused to lose. When that woman stood, her pregnant belly protruded in the dress she wore.

"You will understand in time . . . but for now, sleep."

Nova could not form a simple thought. Her vision was starting to become dark, and her body was going limp. She was a fighter, needed to escape, but the darkness took over and she was now at the mercy of her captors.

*

Layla calmly walked into the library.

"Kace?"

It had been two days since the generals gave his mother's name. They called her Dinah. Rumors that they gave themselves names were verified.

"I grew up knowing my mother left when I was only a few days old. My father said it was to protect us . . ."

His mother was a general and his father a Witch. He would have been defenseless around her. If she claimed him and bore his children, Nova and Kace would have been taken back to Hell. But she left to protect them, which meant there was something he did not understand.

"I can't . . ."

His mind was swimming with questions that didn't have an answer. It was Layla's touch on his face that brought him out of his thoughts. Her fingers gently traced the blind, the king's blessing. Never did Kace allow her to take it off, but this time felt different.

"You are the son of a Hellion general. Your strength and power are known because you have nothing to prove to anyone. I love you; let me protect what I choose to love."

Layla had been patient, but the generals wanted Kace back. She was ready to go to war for Kace to be at her side. Love wouldn't be enough to protect him, and she had an entire world that would fight for the one man who made her feel alive.

"My secrets are not to protect me, but others close to me."

Kace's words caused Layla to frown.

"If you ask me to trust you—"

Layla took a hand away from the blindfold and grabbed his hand. Gently, she placed that hand on her stomach. After they returned to her castle, all they did was sleep. If Kace were to see her, he would have seen her belly was starting to grow.

"You can't claim me, and Hellions can only get pregnant through claims," Kace said out loud, feeling the life growing inside her.

Layla smiled. "I do not know how it happened, but I am a full-blooded Fae. My father was one of the last males. We can only claim non-Hellions and mix our blood to keep our race alive—"

"I am not—"

Layla kept talking. "You are not mortal, and the origin of the generals are unknown. Whatever you are triggered my body's natural ability to conceive, but I will not lose you to this war. I refuse to allow you to put yourself in harm's way."

There was a sigh of defeat before Layla went to take off the king's mark. Kace's body was screaming against this action, but he trusted her. A Hellion, a Fae. He loved her but was too afraid to say it out loud.

"Look at me," she ordered.

Kace closed his eyes the moment she took it off. His heart beat rapidly, but slowly those purple eyes opened, and he looked up at her. To see the woman he loved for the first time with those eyes made emotions flood his face. She was more beautiful than his brain created for him, and when she leaned in, he met her halfway.

The kiss was passionate. Feeling her nails dig into the flesh on his face caused blood to slowly drip down his cheek. His blood was gold to symbolize his immortality and mixed race. Layla already knew the color of his blood, one usually hidden by his dark uniform but those jeweled irises, the golden blood, only one creature had those features.

"Only royalty has golden blood, my love, and the King of Hell is known for his jeweled-red eyes . . ."

Those words didn't register for Kace. Seeing Layla for the first time, it took all he had in him to breathe. For ten years all he knew was violence. This woman was his only light. Everything else felt distant. His mind wasn't thinking about the knowledge that his mother was a Hellion general, or the love of his life was pregnant with his child, or his origins stemmed from the Hellion king himself.

XVIII

"If you invade Fae, it would be seen as the king invading the territory."

Kelby tried to make Vadim understand. They both looked at the map of the Fae world, but no one saw an easy solution in rescuing Kace.

"How could you let the Fae king take your ward?" Hadwin signed.

"If the boy is indeed Dinah's son, she is in more danger than we realized," Everard signed, showing he still couldn't grasp this situation.

All seven generals are forbidden to reproduce. They are not even meant to be seen as more than tools, but behind closed doors, they formed a bond with each other. Five now occupied the room, with one new to this situation. With all of them in one place, it meant the King of Hell didn't want them around.

"We can't leave Dinah alone," Qued signed.

Kelby looked towards Qued.

"You can with Reid, where is he?" he signed.

The general shrugged. "All he told me was there was a mess he needed to clean up."

"It was wise of you not to ask questions," Kelby replied.

"I agree." Qued looked at the others and knew what he had to do.

"I will go back and stay out of sight. It will give me peace of mind to be able to protect her from the king killing her."

"He will track your movements," Hadwin interjected.

Qued nodded. "Which means I will need a reason to go back."

"If you tell him the Fae took Vadim's ward, the king will give permission to invade if the ward is not released," Kelby suggested.

Vadim knew the words were spoken around him, even if he couldn't hear them. Sign language was one of many ways they communicated, but when he looked up, everyone was focused on him.

"He is her key," Vadim began.

"None of us were alive when information about the gatekeepers was accessible. The only one who would know what it meant to have them alive is Reid, but I do not trust Kace in his hands."

Their conversation was cut short when a soldier came into the tent and took a knee. Whispers of the reason so many generals were here led to speculation about a final attack, and when he reported the King of Fae was here, everyone moved with haste.

*

Kace leaned up against the wall across the room, watching Layla pace back and forth. She was ready for battle. Her armor glistened with the light that illuminated the area. Her mind was racing with solutions to protect her world, but when her eyes looked at Kace, her hard expression softened.

He no longer wore the band with the mark of the King of Hell. But it was discussed in detail that his origins needed to remain hidden for the safety of their unborn child. A simple mask hid the truth, but when the generals entered, they noticed he no longer wore any markings of their king. A sign of rebellion.

"Do not mistake my action, generals, my key is mine. No matter the color he wears, he will always be mine. Threaten him again and the Fae will pull from the alliance."

The anger was towards Vadim, the general that for some strange reason Kace still trusted.

"Careful, Your Majesty," Qued signed but Vadim was the one to speak next.

"Our interest lies with the wellbeing of my ward. You cannot take him as long as he claims loyalty to our king." Vadim looked at Kace, making sure the man understood.

"If you strip your band, you will be brought before the king for judgement and be sentenced to death for betrayal."

Kace slowly reached his hand up and removed his mask. All five men watched as for the first time he showed his entire face. Those purple eyes glistened as he blinked. No one seemed surprised that he was a Witch—they all knew he wasn't mortal—but when Kace put the mask on the table, he looked towards Vadim.

"All I asked of you was answers—"

In hearing Kace's words, Vadim went to sign but Kace continued.

"I needed to know who my mother was and in order for me to get that answer, I had to become someone I was not."

"Kace . . .," Vadim signed.

"I will no longer raise a sword in the Hellion king's name and if you choose to bring me before him, I will resist."

His words were calm but inside, Kace was screaming. He didn't want to lose Vadim, the only connection he had with this part of his life. But Layla and his child, they were the most important things to him now. He was ready for a fight, so was Layla, but the generals didn't draw their weapons.

"She mated with a Witch," Kelby signed.

"She could have done worse," Qued replied and walked out of the tent.

One by one they all walked out until it was the three of them. Vadim looked towards Kace but chose to say nothing. He didn't know what to say. If the Fae rebelled, they would join the dozens of worlds that were fighting against the Hellion king. More and more refused to bow to the king's demands, which was why the generals were created. If Kace became the cause of losing the Fae, he would be the most wanted man not only in Hell but also in Heaven.

XIX

A loud scream woke Nova from a dreamless slumber. Her eyes immediately found the wooden ceiling above her head. Flashes of what happened before she was taken by the darkness replayed in her mind.

There was a woman lying on her bed, in the home she hadn't seen in over ten years. There was someone who grabbed Nova from behind. A strong individual who caused her to lose all sense of self.

Nova sat up and looked at her wings. She remembered how heavy they felt, but now she could move them with ease. Another loud scream was followed by a newborn cry. Movement behind the closed door in front of her caught Nova's attention.

"We need more hot water," a voice said from the other side of the door.

Nova moved cautiously out of the bed. She now wore a long green dress, and her hair flowed when she walked. She always tried to hide in the background, but how she looked now made her stand out.

"I got the towels," another voice yelled when she opened the door.

Many females with purple eyes moved up and down the narrow hallway. Sounds of newborn cries made them all move faster. Nova naturally moved with them until she stopped at an open doorway. Movement filled that room, but a woman stopped Nova from advancing, crossing her arms as if protecting someone inside.

142

"Can I help you?" she asked.

The woman was tall, and those purple eyes met Nova with hostility. Markings littered her skin, ancient symbols of moon, hell, and war. Another woman stepped into view, a mirror copy of the one who was ready to tear Nova apart.

"Girls, let her through," a familiar voice called out.

Both women wore clothing associated with the races of Heaven and Hell. Questions started to form, but hearing that voice, the one that belonged to the woman in her home, made those questions immediately disappear. When she saw that woman's face, Nova was still.

"No need to pass out, Nova. Tallia, can you please get her a chair?" the woman asked.

A newborn infant was swaddled in the woman's arms. It moved and tried to cause their mother trouble, but the look she gave was that of love. But it was the face that Nova couldn't look away from, even when she was forced to sit in a chair.

"Your father was the one who told me you ran away in search of your brother. Eddison was vague on the details but suspected you would go home first. You are safe here, dear, never fear what you do not understand."

The woman's face, it was her father's face. An identical image. He had a sister, a twin that neither she nor Kace knew about. Why would he keep that from them? Nova's eyes looked at the infant in the woman's arms and then to the two bassinets next to her bed. Twins. Even the two women glaring at Nova from behind were twins, redheaded twins.

"Why didn't he tell me?" Nova signed, finally able to form a thought.

"To not only protect you but my family as well," the woman replied.

"I don't understand," Nova signed.

143

"When Eddison and I were born, our father knew if two red-haired twins were discovered, the risk of a gatekeeper rumor may start. There was no other choice, we had to be separated. Our mother kept him while our father took me."

She had to stop, only for a moment. They were no older than her newborns. It had been so long ago, but it still hurt as if it happened yesterday. But she knew she had to continue for Nova to understand.

"It was a painful day, but we always knew the other existed. They never stopped us from communicating with each other, so when he disappeared for nineteen years, I grew worried."

The infant in her arms struggled and Nova saw the wings on its back. When she turned to look at the adult twins, one of them winked.

"The binding spell can be controlled with practice. That is why my daughter's wings are not visible. It isn't safe for those with black-feathered wings," the woman explained.

The woman shifted uncomfortably. Nova remembered the feeling after giving birth. How the body slowly started to feel tired and sore. She needed to rest. Nova stood, but those two women appeared at her side, not letting her go anywhere without permission.

"I need you both to stay here until your father returns."

They didn't argue but knew better than to speak because their mother was not finished.

"Now that we found your cousin, we need to find her brother before the Hellions do."

There was a plan being formed that left Nova at their mercy. One of the women grabbed her arm and forced her out of the room. Nova knew better than to fight, she was outnumbered, but her eyes fell to the windows in the hallway showing the snow-covered mountains in the distance.

"Make sure we were not followed," one of the women said and Nova looked back at her.

They may share the same face, but the woman in white seemed to whisper to the air. Her movements caused a chill to cover Nova's skin.

"I am not babysitting. You can deal with this . . .," the one wearing black and covered in facial markings muttered.

She vanished in a wave of smoke and fire, leaving Nova with the other woman who didn't seem pleased her sister vanished.

"Bitch . . ."

It was too much. This place was unfamiliar and filled with people she didn't know. Nova was led into a large sitting room, and the woman finally let her arm go.

"Where am I?" Nova signed when the woman looked at her.

Nova had no idea if the woman knew sign language, but how she didn't seem irritated with the form of communication gave Nova a hint of hope she was understood.

"Don't worry about it. What is your name?"

Nova signed her name.

"Nova . . . hmm . . ."

With a wave of her hand, the woman in white's black wings appeared. She spread them high and wide to demonstrate power. It wasn't just the wings that changed, her purple eyes seemed to glimmer, like hers. Everything about her seemed to be familiar to Nova.

"Your father fell for a general too," the woman began.

Nova didn't form a word, she listened.

"There is only one female general of Hell, which means we are not only cousins through our Wiccan blood but our royal blood as well."

145

Nova felt a pressure that caused her to fall over. An invisible force pushed her down to a ground created by nothing. The entire room disappeared, and all sense of space was gone. When Nova sat up, strong arms wrapped around her, and rather than fight, Nova leaned into the embrace. She recognized the person that held her.

"Never again will you run from me," Navar whispered.

Nova held back the tears that threatened to fall.

"If you need something or are worried, you come to me, and only me. Do you understand?"

Nova turned to look at him. Navar was not only her king, but he was also her love, her husband, and the father of her children. She wanted to be strong, but right now, Nova was terrified of everything changing around her.

"You are the key to the Dragons, who would have thought," the red-haired woman said, and both Navar and Nova looked at her.

She no longer wore a long white flowing gown. Golden chains hung from her hips and ears and a golden hairpiece weaved into her long red locks. A man stood beside her, wearing a white suit. He didn't seem intimidating, but when Nova looked into his eyes, they were nothing but a void, one that caused fear to crawl over her body.

"I brought you here, Navar, not only to show you that your wife was safe but to discuss important business. None of your souls will be harmed if you choose to talk here, but if the mortal—"

Navar did not want Nova in this world any longer.

"Release us!" he demanded.

"Very well . . ."

Nova sat up in the library gasping for air. Being in that place felt like she was drowning, but Navar walked up behind her and picked her up. Nova didn't care if he was mad or how Navar found her, but she needed him. Holding onto him tightly, her eyes found the same redheaded

146

woman standing in the distance, but the man standing to her side felt like nothing more than a ghost.

"Seemed you and I not only found our keys but a wife as well," the man said.

Navar held onto Nova tightly.

"We want nothing to do with your rebellion," Navar stated but the redhead only smiled at the statement.

"Your wife running away from your protection means she does not trust in your ability or Mora's. She came to us for answers, even if she didn't know the question that needed to be asked."

That woman held confidence laced with cockiness, and when Nova tried to defend her husband, Navar spoke instead.

"What do you want?" he demanded.

The woman laughed. She was carefree now that the man was with her. That guarded expression faded, and Nova dared to think she was enjoying this little conversation.

"Your help."

Navar growled. "We are enemies—"

The man who was silent the entire time finally spoke. His voice brought silence to the room and demanded everyone's attention.

"We are united. Not only by our ideals or the love we have for our people, but through our wives. All the texts about the gatekeepers have been lost, but the souls that lived since then hold the knowledge. Did you know, Navar, that gatekeepers come in pairs? Always two, and always on opposing sides."

Navar looked over to Nova but then to the woman who appeared in the distance. The woman held the same face, but it was the man who appeared at her side, a creature with eyes glowing a deep red and darkness wrapping

147

around his legs. His ears were pointed, and his skin was like endless night.

"Raynar."

The man smirked. "Who would have thought you'd rebel against your king, Navar. You always had a knack for being obedient."

"I am not rebelling."

The man shrugged.

"You could have fooled me," he teased.

"If both of you are here with your keys, it means you are ready to attack."

Navar wasn't an idiot; he knew who these two men were. One of the Heavens and another of Hell. He dared not speak of their affiliations, but it was obvious they both were here of their own free will, and it seemed, no matter what Navar tried to do, he was outnumbered.

"Enough!" a third woman shouted.

Everyone's eyes looked towards her. It was the woman who shared Eddison's face, the one who gave birth a few hours ago. She looked agitated and in pain, but her attention was fully on the men who hadn't come to a mutual understanding.

"We need to work together. As kings, I expect all of you gentlemen to come together over rip each other apart. If you choose to stay in my home, you will abide by my rules. My husband will return at nightfall; I suggest you all wait until then so our differences can be settled."

She was strong, but when the twins ran to her side, it seemed she needed the aid of her children to avoid hurting herself further. The men who occupied the room were kings of their own realms. Both of Heaven and Hell, the Kings of Dragon, Demon, and Spirit. Enemies of yesterday, but today, they stood in one place ready not to destroy but to protect the ones they loved.

XX

"What do you mean, the Fae have taken the ward?" the King of Hell yelled as Qued knelt before him.

"My King," Qued signed, keeping his eyes to the ground.

"Upon returning to the camp, the Fae had invaded. The chaos created an opportunity to overpower the ward and take him. They are demanding an audience to negotiate his release."

The king did not speak. Anger was evident in his gaze. He could only see those who hold his mark in the Mortal world. By the ward having the mark removed, and the generals being in one place, he was blind to the truth. He hated relying solely on the individual reports over the knowledge he already knew.

"Why are you here and not invading Fae?" he yelled, and Qued showed no reaction.

"The Fae are women. A man cannot cross into their world."

He sighed. It didn't take the king long to understand the way the generals could communicate. The curse of the Fae was something he had caused. It was a way to keep them loyal through fear. No man should be born from a Fae to avoid a rebellion and an uprising.

"She is banned from leaving the castle, find another way," he grumbled.

The only female general was never to leave his sight.

The castle was vast, and when Qued was dismissed, no one followed the general as he walked down the halls. All the servants bowed out of fear, knowing that he was loyal to the king. For over two hundred years the generals had existed, and no one remembered a world without them.

Qued frowned when he finally appeared in front of a cell. He could smell her from a distance, not only the odor her body created but the dried blood that littered the hallways. Dinah. She was chained to the walls, covered in lash marks, burns, and healing cuts. She was beaten multiple times a day, depending on the king's mood, for a crime of which she already paid the price. But, by hiding her here, the world would never be able to feel pity for her.

Qued looked side to side. No one was allowed to come down here, but that didn't mean someone wasn't watching. When he felt he was truly alone, he opened the cage and took a step forward. Her eyes were covered by a blood-stained cloth, and her mouthpiece was violently removed. Pain. It was the only word he could think of.

He reached forward and started to undo the chains. Dinah slowly moved her head up but didn't make a sound. She knew it was him, someone that wasn't going to hurt her, and she fell easily into his arms, limp and struggling to find the will to fight. If those she was trying to protect were safe there was no reason for her to fight back.

*

"You will be the next punching bag by taking her without permission," Kelby signed.

Qued was able to take Dinah away from her cage to a place where she could heal. She slept soundly in a bed surrounded by five generals who looked at her with worry. They knew she was being beaten, but they didn't expect it to be to this extreme. Never was the king emotional, but what he did to her showed he was rageful and out of control.

"As long as Reid stays away, she will be fine," Vadim signed.

Dinah moved in her sleep. Little noises escaped her lips, and she would vomit and scream. Sound was never heard from her lips by them, and it scared them. But she was safe; her body recognized she was safe and allowed her defenses to slowly come down.

"We will be watching her in turns to avoid suspicion," Hadwin signed, and they all agreed.

The generals were bred for destruction, to follow an order, and to be a tool for war. Never were they allowed to think, to feel, so to have them protect one of their own showed they were evolving beyond the king's control. Which meant, the world would feel the shift and a change was about to come forth.

XXI

Men were never seen in Fae; it was almost forbidden to speak of them within their walls. Whispers started to spread of a man walking in the halls of the castle, where no man was allowed to be.

"It can't be true."

"I saw him with my own eyes! He was in the castle."

"If a man is here, does that mean we are under attack?"

"A man? In the castle?"

The guards and servants whispered. It followed Layla's ears, and she tried desperately to ignore it. But the whispers were loud enough that she heard them through the doors of her war room. It went from the shock of a man being in the castle, to what clothes he was wearing.

"I spoke to a servant of the tailor. They swear the measurements were for a man's body."

The woman giggled as they passed the door.

"Rumor is also starting that an allied force is coming. Maybe they will bring some attractive men with them."

Layla groaned to herself and held back the need to roll her eyes. She hated gossip but it couldn't be helped. In the protection of the night, Kace brought in his army and hid them within the forest. His soldiers were loyal to him and trained to follow without question. The need to please was a failsafe built into their creation, but the lack of free will bothered Kace.

"With General Kace now in our alliance, not only had our armies increased in number but our chances of survival have become greater," one of Layla's generals reported.

"But?" she mumbled, feeling another part of the statement needed to be said.

"The rising eighth general is a follower of the Hellion king. They all are born and raised to fight for him. This could be—"

"Have the soldiers settled?" Layla asked in a whisper, no longer listening to the conversation in front of her.

A hand was over her mouth to show her intention but to hide her speech. They didn't need to have her involved, but she needed to be present to mediate. Her other hand was hidden from view, interlocked behind the chair with the man who had yet to leave her side.

Kace only smirked at the question. He sat behind her high-back chair, out of sight but still close. His eyes were covered with a deep-blue cloth. Even though he was fully truthful to Layla, the need to hide his blood was still a priority. Rumors were the fuel to anyone's demise.

"I am talking to you . . .," she muttered.

Kace wore her colors, deep blue with green intertwined in the fabric. His hair was red and vibrant against the colors, but the pants, vest, and boots all matched the color scheme of this realm. He fully declared his allegiance to Layla and wasn't afraid to show it.

"Considering all two-hundred-and-fifty-thousand male soldiers are seeing women for the first time, I say they are fine," he responded playfully.

"Should I be worried?" Layla replied.

He chuckled. "They are obedient, but the moment I grant them free will, I will need to implement rules for everyone's protection."

"Will they still be loyal if free will is granted?"

Free will was something all creations of Hell would never achieve. They were a tool, and once they are no longer useful, they would be destroyed. But, for his soldiers, he would grant them the freedom of choice and help them adapt to a world they never thought was possible.

"I am all they know, and they will obey. Did you agree to be my wife because of the baby?" Kace asked.

A child was growing inside her, his child, and Layla still did not know how it was possible. The Hellion king's curse was preventing everyone from bearing a child unless it was through a claim. She couldn't claim Kace due to his Hellion blood, but that child was real, her love for him was real.

"I would have said yes regardless," she began and switched topics.

"There needs to be a full count of all soldiers. Both mine and yours. By you accepting me as your wife and me accepting you as my gatekeeper, I am not part of the rebellion against the king. I want no surprises."

"I didn't hear a please," Kace teased.

"I am your king, and you will follow my commands."

Kace knew the conversation around them was still going on. When he stood, all generals were stunned. Someone was in the room they didn't know was there. They all went to attack, but when Kace took their king's hand and kissed it, the confusion was evident on their faces.

"Say please," Kace said loud enough for them to hear. "Now."

Kace only smiled but walked out of the room. Layla's generals saw his colors, but when they saw his wings, the color vanished from their faces. They knew what it meant to have blacked-feathered wings, and to have one of them here was terrifying.

"Get me a count of all soldiers," Kace ordered one of his soldiers, who was waiting for him in the hallway.

"Contact General Vadim and ask for an update. He will know what it means."

Kace's soldier bowed his head and walked away. The Fae was cursed to only give birth to women through claim. Claiming was a practice Kace did not enjoy. But he needed to talk to the only person he knew that may know how to break a curse, one set by the same man they were all meant to serve.

XXII

Night had fallen on the mountainside overlooking the coven. An hour ago, a man walked into the house to hold his sleeping wife. No one knew he was there except his four grown children who were trained to find him in case they needed his help.

"Father?" a man whispered as he slowly walked into the bedroom.

The woman, the twin of Nova's father, lay snuggled against a man in familiar clothing. One of his hands held the woman he loved, and the other was in the bassinet as his newborns slept peacefully while their father felt the rise and fall of their chests.

"Who is our plus two?" he asked quietly.

His armor glistened the deep colors of Hell, which was where he was created. The man's short white hair was part of a picture that associated him with seven deadly creatures. Reid. The first general to be created, the strongest and the most feared, had the biggest secret of all. His mask and eye cover were removed, and his eyes never left his wife but waited for the answer he sought from his grown son.

"Dragon King Navar and his queen," the man replied.

None of the generals spoke. If they did, a secret would be revealed. An Angel has a calming voice: it soothes the mind and creates a peace. It was an unneeded skill in battle, but all the generals had a layer of calm in their voice, and Reid used it to keep his infant sons asleep.

"Your brother?" the general asked.

"No word. A general's army was sent to detain them." Reid was not worried about that fact.

"I already took care of it. I want you to wait with your sisters and summon me when he arrives," he ordered, and his son bowed before walking out of the room.

*

"Stop staring," a cheerful woman called out to Navar, who followed her movements around the library.

When that woman walked in, Navar went silent. His eyes never left her. It wasn't because of her beauty or her golden hair that fell so perfectly past her shoulders. The green dress held the golden designs of the Elves, but those creatures were part of the Heaven alliance until they broke apart and joined the rebellion a hundred years ago.

"You are no longer outnumbered, Willow. Another Heaven-sent realm has come to their senses," Raynar, the Demon king, teased.

"I am still loyal to my king, unlike someone . . ."

Navar only spoke those few words before the door opened. The man that walked in had hair of fire like the twins in the room, and like the twins, his features were hidden by magic. The Elven king looked excited to see him and ran over to greet him on a more personal level.

"What about Arc?" the woman dressed in white asked as the King of Spirits roamed around the room.

"Cleaning up a mess."

"Father?"

"With Mother and the boys," he replied, but his eyes found Nova, and when she finally saw him, he took a step back.

"Ash?" Nova signed, confused by seeing a familiar face in this place.

"Nova?"

Navar looked from his wife to the man.

"You two know each other?" he asked.

Nova stood quickly, and before Navar could grab her, she ran over to Ash with haste and punched him hard across the face. They all could hear the crunch of the bones. Everyone froze in place and watched Nova summon a golden sword.

She made a sacrifice, her voice, to wield the holy weapon. By drawing it now, she showed the interaction between the two wasn't a pleasant one. Armor covered her body. It glistened with the mark of the Heaven king, and the action she was about to take showed the sword was going to be lethal.

"So, it is true. Your wife is a soldier in Her Majesty's army," the Demon king whispered to Navar.

It happened in an instant. When Nova went to attack, a man appeared with his own sword drawn. No one moved to help Ash or Nova; they couldn't. Something was holding them in place.

That man had the same face as the man on the ground, but his expression was calm and understanding. As Nova spread her wings, a woman appeared behind her and pushed Nova forward, causing her to fall on her face.

The force holding everyone in place was from the magic the building cast to protect those who lived within, but Nova was not affected because the blood she shared held the key to make the freedom of choice. But movement behind her felt familiar, and she was bound once more by a device that made her body feel heavy.

"Am I to assume you are the individual who found my son spying in the Heavens and almost killed him if I hadn't intervened?" the voice said.

Navar struggled against the hold. His power as a king put him at a greater level than any coven cast could hold, but it took all the kings in the room to hold him back. When he spoke, Navar's body calmed, but his brain was screaming. His wife had her wings locked in a device and the sword bound to her soul lay motionless in her hands.

"Based on your lack of response, my assumption is correct. For you to be able to track and wound my child shows your strength and skill."

Nova tried to move, tried to form a thought, but his voice kept her in a state of bliss. One that rendered her helpless.

"It doesn't matter if you are blood, I will kill you if you harm what is mine. Withdraw your sword and deactivate your armor."

159

One of the seven generals, deadly and feared. Hearing his voice confused Nova and Navar. It was Angelic, and his ability to calm the room created an unnecessary fear in all those who didn't understand. When he finally let Nova stand, she looked at him and could not look away.

His eyes glistened like jewels but were bright red like the Hellion kings were rumored to be. Only that creature had eyes such as these, and before Nova raised her hands to ask, Reid reached out and touched the top of her head.

"You are welcomed to stay if you need. All the answers will be given to you in time, but I need you to keep my secret to protect what is dear to me."

Nova nodded and Reid continued.

"You are free to return to your realm, but be warned, if the Dragons join the rebellion, you will lose your sword. Mora does not forgive betrayal."

Rebellion. Kings of realms once under Hell and Heaven chose to break free of their protection. The strength of both worlds lay in their allies, and both were slowly starting to lose them all.

XXIII

Every battle fought stained the ground red. It had been red for as long as the world could remember. It happened long before the generals came into existence, and with the fall of the last Hellion city in the Mortal world, Dinah finally opened her eyes.

A bounty was on her head. There was no official report like the one on Qued, but she knew that going back to Hell was out of the question if she wanted to live. Her soldiers were given to the rising eighth general. Each soul was wiped and reprogrammed to follow their new leader, leaving Dinah defenseless. If it wasn't for the remaining generals sheltering her, she wouldn't be alive.

"There is not much left, we need to keep moving," Qued signed to her.

Dinah walked over the rubble of what used to be her home. No structure survived the final attack, not even the protected ones. The flames of Hell no longer existed here, and when she moved aside some rubble, she found what she was looking for.

It was a small silver chest that she held tightly to her body. Ignoring Qued's eagerness to leave, she moved slowly back to the place she had been hiding. Dinah was

161

so afraid it would break, that this small box would disappear if she moved too fast or let go. When she appeared in her room, she finally let a tear escape.

Eddison. Dinah had been thinking about him ever since she had woken up. This box, it was one of the few gifts he gave to her during that year they had together. He called it a memory box, and he told her that every milestone their children had he would capture in a picture. The small things that reminded him of them, he would add to the box. This box was a comfort for Dinah because when she was in Hell, she needed to hide that year away so the king could not take them from her, and knowing this box existed made her feel less disconnected.

Only she and Eddison knew how to open the box. It was a puzzle. A few items moved which opened a few points that needed to be pressed. It was simple but delicate and when she opened that box, she saw two small dolls that were no bigger than her palm. One was dressed in a red shirt and the other a red dress, and both were worn from love.

Dinah was used to hiding her face, but her white hair fell from the dark hood she hid behind. A small smile crossed her lips. When she lifted those dolls, a photograph was there showing two newborn babies sleeping peacefully side by side.

Nova. Kace. She could still smell their scent and feel the softness of their skin. So much time was lost, but those few days she could hold them meant everything to her.

A picture for every birthday. Dinah watched them grow from birth to their nineteenth year. Those infants shared the same face but had personalities that were different. The last picture, the one when they were all grown up, showed them both sitting on a counter. Nova had her hair long and wild, the same color as her brother and father, and she held a food item in her hand. By the anger-filled expression, Dinah could only assume the argument was about a meal.

But her eyes saw the symbol of the Dragon king across her daughter's chest. The dress she wore was low cut and the design was unique to that one race. It was a claim, but from a Heaven-sent clan. Why would the Dragons claim her?

Dinah made sure no one knew her attachment to the children. Kace had knives attached to his belt, and his short-sleeved shirt showed his faded scars. They were both supposed to be protected, but it looked like fate had found them. But, if Nova was a captive of the Dragons, Dinah needed to save her.

"You have pictures?" Vadim signed when Dinah looked towards him.

She tried to collect them quickly, but Vadim was able to grab the one from their nineteenth birthday and walk a few steps away. He showed no shock at the idea of her having children, but his eye fell to Nova. He only knew about Kace, and the twin with the Dragon mark created a concerned expression on his face.

"Please give it back," Dinah whispered.

In her recovery, her mask was removed, which meant her voice returned. It had been weeks since she was rescued, giving her body time to heal, but she still felt uncomfortable using her voice. For some strange reason,

Vadim felt responsible for her, and he had been the only one to hear her speak.

"I haven't met your daughter, but your son, Kace, I had the pleasure of training for the past ten years. He is a strong boy and will make you proud," he signed after handing Dinah back the photo.

The shock in what she learned was evident on her face.

"Are you telling me my son is the rising eighth general?"

Dinah's voice cracked when she tried to speak louder.

"Was," Vadim responded, easing her worry.

"Not only does your son have your soldiers, but he is supported by his wife and her army. You will be proud of the man he is now—"

"Wife?"

Vadim stopped his hands and knew that he had information that she was not ready for. The gentleness he felt towards her wasn't because she was the youngest general amongst them or because she was a woman. She did something all generals wanted to do but did not have the courage. Her choices saved someone close to all of them, and they all swore to always protect her.

Without another word, he handed her a letter before he made his exit. Dinah waited until she was alone to slowly open the parchment. It was written in a mortal language, one she assumed Vadim and her son used for a more private conversation. But thankfully, she knew it too

Vadim:

All is well.

You always told me to start with that for you to feel at ease. Now you cannot yell at me for not starting this properly. I have settled in and appreciate you still checking in on me.

I know you do not need the details, and sadly, I cannot give you them, but know that I am happy. Both my wife and unborn child are strong and healthy. I am also staying out of trouble to the best of my ability, and remember, old man, you promised to help me find my mother. I expect you to do well on that promise.

Be well.

Kace

A promise. Vadim had promised to help find her. Why would her son want to find her? She left both of her children crying in their beds to protect them. Where was their father? Why would he allow the children to get involved in the war? All Dinah knew was Vadim had the knowledge of where he was, and she was going to find him.

XXIV

"The doctor said I am five months along, but because of how tall I am, I didn't start showing until recently."

Layla had been hiding her pregnancy for as long as she could. She was not ashamed but knew it would make situations more complicated. Layla found comfort in isolation and when she lay down on a couch in the library, she felt her husband's warm body near her.

"Has the gossip about you and I turned?" Kace teased.

Layla only smiled. The two armies integrated with ease. But since the moment Kace gave them free will, there had been a few incidents of men and women being caught in each other's beds. This was a world full of women, a temptation that any man would risk.

"I am banging the new general is the newest one I am hearing. But the statements are not true, a little vulgar for my taste."

He smiled at his wife.

"I thought you liked vulgarity?"

Layla couldn't help but chuckle.

"I want everyone to stop talking about it and focus on the matter at hand."

"Which is?" Kace asked, knowing she was in a playful mood.

"None of my clothing fits," she grumbled.

Kace laughed and slowly moved to be able to kiss her stomach.

*

Fae were magic users cursed by gender. Fae focused on the power that was beyond the elements, one the naked eye could not see. They drew the power from the stars, but Dinah used her own strength to sneak into the Fae world after she got to where her son was hiding. Her experience in war got her to this point, but how she would approach her son terrified her.

The soldiers that walked the grounds were a mix between her own and the Fae. Their programming was wired to her command, but she noticed that they moved around freely with no structure or guidance. Did Kace give them free will?

A black cloak hid her small frame, the black dress she wore aided her ability to move in the darkness, and out of habit, she wore a black cloth over her eyes. This castle, it was grand, but she could feel him, the one man she hadn't seen in over thirty years.

"Stop."

The command Kace gave in the distance caused Dinah to freeze in her tracks. The Fae did not have the type of magic to track her, not even Eddison, but the other generals can track darkness. Dinah should have expected that of the eighth general.

"You are trespassing. State your business," Kace demanded when Dinah did not turn around.

What should she say to him? Her identifying marks were hidden, including her wings, and Kace was walking closer. Not alerting the nearby guards meant he was going to deal with her on his own. Foolish boy.

When Kace went to grab her shoulder, Dinah moved swiftly and grabbed his arm. Even though Kace could track her, she was still faster. With ease, Dinah grabbed his arm and pinned him against the wall.

When Kace expanded his wings, her own wings moved and pinned them, expanded and exposed. How she pinned them was between the feathers, not to damage the tendons. When Kace went to draw his sword, she placed her foot on the hilt and forced it back in.

Kace went to speak; Dinah covered his mouth with her hand. White locks fell from her hood but when Kace saw her face, he saw she looked like Nova. No, she had Nova's face shape, his too, and same nose, but the black fabric covering her eyes was an indication.

Black wings, white hair, eyes of jewels hidden behind the cloth. Only one female general existed, and that general was who he was looking for.

"Mother?" he asked weakly as a wave of energy was sent towards them.

When that energy got closer, Dinah removed one of her wings and blocked the attack. Her eyes found the Fae king at the end of the hall. When Layla went to attack again, Kace broke free of his mother's hold and got in between the two women.

169

"Stop!" Kace yelled.

Dinah jumped over her son to advance, but he grabbed her leg and pulled her towards him.

"I said stop!" he yelled once more.

Layla growled towards her husband's outburst. When Dinah kicked him away, her hood fell. Everyone was silent, only looking at each other. Layla. There were no longer any secrets between the two, and when Dinah turned to Kace, Dinah did without saying a word and grabbed his arm, leading him towards a sitting room. Layla did not follow.

"Mother—" Kace began. Dinah pinned him once more to the wall, but this time, his back was exposed.

Kace gasped when Dinah forced his wings apart. She spread her hand against the joints, the feathers, and the bone, from stem to tip, stretching and finding the aggravated muscles.

"If you only use your wings as a shield and for speed, they will not be able to support your body in flight. These muscles are not supposed to be tight," she whispered.

Kace was overwhelmed with emotion. He moved his face against the wall to hide the tears that escaped. This moment Kace had waited for his entire life, but he knew not what to say.

Once Dinah checked his wings, she turned him around and finally saw his face without looking through a picture. Like her, his eyes were covered, but when Dinah lowered her head and rested it against his chest, the strength she had vanished.

"I am sorry. I tried to protect the three of you and I failed," she whispered.

Seeing her son's face, she couldn't be strong. He was tall like his father and built like a warrior. But she could not understand how her child could fall into the one path she never wanted for him.

Noise in the distance caused Kace to meet the eyes of his wife. She walked into the room slowly. Her being here meant she knew who this woman was. More importantly, knew what this woman meant to him.

"Generals," Layla said calmly.

Dinah got tense in hearing someone enter the room, but Kace wrapped his strong arms around his mother, making sure she didn't attack.

"Rounds are in thirty minutes. I expect both of you to be there," Layla ordered.

Kace nodded, watching Layla walk out of the room.

"I know you do not know me, Mother. You and I are more similar than you would like. I am happy you are here, but please be patient."

Dinah held onto Kace's shirt.

"I won't leave you again, I promise."

Kace only nodded, holding onto his mother. There would be time for the two to talk. By Layla giving a command, it seemed the Fae approved of Dinah being in their realm, and he could use his mother's help in keeping the soldiers under control.

XXV

"Where is Dinah?" Reid signed when he appeared in Vadim's camp.

It had been months since Dinah woke up and went to find Kace. Vadim received no communication from either person, but that did not worry him. Between hiding Qued and the Heaven-sent advancement, he had been busy. When Reid appeared in the middle of his troop formation, he knew this conversation was unavoidable.

"You asking means she isn't where she belongs," Vadim signed but focused on his troops.

All the generals feared Reid. He not only was the eldest and strongest, but his word held as much weight as the Hellion king's. Vadim failed in hiding Dinah. With Reid here, he showed he suspected something.

"And Qued?" Reid asked.

"He was supposed to report the issue of the Fae to our

king. I have not seen him since. Is there something I can do for you, Reid?"

Reid did not reply. He walked away, but Vadim watched nervously. When Reid spread his wings, flying high above, Vadim knew they all were in trouble. Reid's army was the only one they could not see. They were created for the sneak attack, one that Reid was known to do successfully.

"General," one of his soldiers reported when Reid landed.

He knew they were hiding Dinah and Qued. The generals were smart, but there was a reason he was the strongest. Reid walked into the sleeping quarters of Vadim and started to look around.

Vadim was a creature of habit and needed to write everything down. Each piece of paper was written in shorthand and illegible, but after tearing apart every stack, he found a communication from his ward. Everyone had been calling him the rising eighth general. Reid wanted to meet him, and his being gone for so long without a word caused concern.

The language written was in a mortal dialect. Living for many centuries made language second nature. When Vadim took a ward, something changed. The change had slowly been rippling in all directions and caused the need to investigate.

"Report," Reid said from underneath his mask.

"We found her," his solder replied.

"Where?"

"Fae. The individual you sent to observe the newly rebellious king spotted her former army and a soldier matching her description."

Reid put down the papers.

"Heaven has their sight on Fae along with Kelby's unit. I need you to distract Kelby while I observe the interaction with Heaven," he ordered, and his soldier vanished.

Reid's eyes looked at a letter. One simple piece of paper showing lighthearted banter between two comrades. He refused to leave the evidence behind. Putting it in his pocket, he vanished only to appear on a mountainside not too far from Vadim's camp.

When his phone vibrated in his pocket, he took it out. Technology was a mortal instrument, and generals were forbidden to use it. But when Reid opened it, an image of his youngest boys looked back at him. The pictures on his phone of his family helped him deal with the separation. He saw it was his wife and he answered it.

"You should be sleeping" was his only greeting, knowing what time it was back at the coven house.

"How is Mister Grumpy Pants?" his wife responded.

"My dear Selene, I am not grumpy."

She laughed and that sound was music to his ears.

"I do not believe you but will interrogate you later. Ash dropped by for a quick visit—"

"What happened?" Reid demanded, his mind immediately going on the defense.

"Hush. He wanted me to tell you that the woman is part of the Heaven's army. The details he will report to you directly, but I suspected you wanted to know sooner rather than later."

"I told them not to relay messages through you. I will speak to the children—"

Selene was not having any of this.

"Listen, Mister Grumpy Pants. Have you forgotten that I am their mother, and their secrets are safe with me? I love you, Reid, and always will. No matter where this war takes you, you have a home, a family, and my heart. Never forget that."

Selene knew Reid could never hang up the phone. He clung to her words because of what he had to endure. When the call ended, Reid looked back to the pictures of his sons. Their jeweled-purple eyes looked directly at him, so full of life and love.

He understood why Dinah was so desperately trying to find her son, but danger came with being connected to a Hellion general. The only way he learned to keep his family safe was to keep his distance, but it was getting harder and harder to say goodbye to them.

XXVI

There were three planes to this world, all had their own realms and battles. Hell. Mortal. Heaven. All relied on each other, but to refuse an alliance was to avoid seeming weak. Heaven was no different, and when Eddison found Mora, he was blocked by her soldiers from advancing.

"Where is my daughter?" he demanded.

Mora looked out to her soldiers but acknowledged her gatekeeper.

"You may be a mortal gatekeeper, but you are in my world. If you do not treat me with the respect I deserve, I will throw you into a cell."

Eddison struggled to get closer, but her soldiers refused entry to the balcony she stood on.

"She is—"

Mora interrupted him.

"Nova bowed down to me," she said and finally turned to face him.

"I granted her my power for her loyalty. Regardless of her marriage, she is mine and always will be."

The anger was laced in her voice. Before Eddison could make another demand, Navar broke down the door and pushed the guards away. He was furious.

"Release her from your command!" Navar demanded.

Mora turned her back to both men, void of all emotion. Her soldiers flew by, and once they did, she glanced over to the angry king. His abilities were blocked in Heaven, so was Eddison's magic. In a sense they were both defenseless, but she knew not to underestimate them.

She didn't respond. The words were too much to speak out loud. All she did was spread her golden wings and join her soldiers. War was unavoidable, and it seemed for the first time, Heaven was attacking first.

"Take your hands off of me!" Navar sneered towards the guards who grabbed him.

He went to attack, but the entire room filled with Mora's guards, became silent, and those soldiers' fell unconscious to the floor. Both men turned to see Ash leaning against the wall, amused at their struggle. In that redhead's hand was an Elven blow dart, one that caused the men to fall to the floor.

"You are not supposed to be causing trouble, Navar," he teased.

He wore green pants and a matching shirt. Brown leather straps held them up with charms marking them of Elven origin. Those purple eyes looked towards Eddison, who was confused but not defensive towards this new individual.

"Your woman seems to be fighting for the wrong king," Ash said, and Navar growled.

"She will never again be called upon by Mora. What are you doing here?"

Ash stretched his arms and his wings spread wide. The playful expression was still splashed across his face, but his attention was fully on Navar, leaving Eddison time to study the man before them.

"The misses told me to come. Just because she is part of the rebellion doesn't mean she lost access to Heaven. If I hadn't, you would be in a different situation and not going after the woman who is the key in stopping everything,"

Navar was snapped out of his rage and rushed out the door. Ash was right. He needed to get to Nova, and with what Mora had planned, there wasn't much time to spend arguing.

Eddison still did not know what to say. The black wings and jeweled irises...he knew his sister had children but never met them before. It was as she explained in her letters. Wings of night and eyes that glistened. She mated with a general too.

"Stop gawking, Uncle. Mother asked me to find you and rescue your weak ass." Ash held up his hands defensively.

"Her words, not mine. Shall we?" he asked.

Eddison tried to move, but there was a pull on his leg that kept him in place. There was an anklet on his leg, which held an invisible chain to this realm, this building. Eddison would have left in a heartbeat to go back to his children if he could, but he was a prisoner to his king.

Ash frowned when Eddison didn't move, but he turned to look at his mother who walked into the room. Selene and Eddison were separated at birth and lived different lives. Seeing her in person and feeling her warm embrace—all Eddison could do was hold her tightly and pray this wasn't a dream.

"My son is strong and in doing me this favor, I can rescue my baby brother," she said playfully and finally let him go.

"You do not know who was born first," Eddison replied and watched her movements.

"Your letters helped me feel connected to you and Mother. But you are a prisoner of your king—"

"Mora is not my king," Eddison interrupted coldly.

"Nor is Nobu mine."

When silence filled the space, Eddison spoke.

"Your son looks good, which one is he?"

Selene drew a dagger from her belt and knelt in front of her brother.

"You will see. Let's get you out of here."

The dagger she held was one commonly associated with the generals. Its black-jeweled handle showed its origin. She cut through the anklet with that dagger, and for the first time, Eddison was free. There were no secrets between them, but when Ash appeared behind Eddison, he grabbed the back of his shirt to bring him to a place where he could finally be free of Mora's control.

*

"What do you want to do about the Dragon king?" Ash asked, dropping Eddison in the middle of the library.

179

They were instantly back at the coven house, using Ash's ability as gatekeeper to travel between realms. This was one of the abilities gatekeepers had, but the strength and ability to be undetected Eddison knew the boy got from his father.

"Your father will watch out for him. Go home, do not make Willow wait," she said, and Ash nodded.

When they were alone, she looked down to her brother, who was still processing everything going on around him. He was confused, collecting his bearings. After she helped him stand, Selene motioned for her brother to follow.

Eddison went without protest. His eyes went to the framed parchment and paintings that lined the hallway. It was a sister coven to the moon clan, a connection to a mother she never knew. Eddison's eyes fell to the mountains in the distance, and he frowned.

"Ash and Arc. Malla and Tallia. Your children are what? Fifty and one hundred?" Eddison asked.

Both of their parents were dead. Their mother from old age, and their father from protecting Selene during a Hellion attack. In the beginning they were alone, but they had each other, even if it was from far away.

"Close. Yours are what, over thirty?" she asked.

"Yes."

Eddison watched Selene move closer to him and gently put a hand on his chest.

"I came to find you because I needed my brother. Things are getting out of hand, and my husband needs help, even if he is too stubborn to admit it."

180

Eddison kept his focus on the mountains in the distance.

"I am nothing more than a simple doctor. My children are far more impressive than I am."

"Their mother?" Selene asked.

Eddison never talked about Dinah. Not even to his sister. He did not reply to her question, but when the sounds of infants crying in the distance were heard, Selene moved, and he followed.

"We have a duty, Eddison. You and I are the only ones able to create gatekeepers. The more that exists, the more this world has a chance for peace."

Eddison looked at the two fussy infants in the bassinet.

"Kace and Nova were a gift. I do not know where their mother is, or if she even cares enough to come back."

Selene picked up Mica, trying not to upset his brother Lee, and gently put him in Eddison's arms.

"I had the pleasure of meeting Nova. A free-spirited little thing. By her wings and eyes, it suggested her mother is the female Hellion general. How did that happen?" she asked, watching Eddison take her son to the chair near the window.

"I was walking to work one day and stumbled upon a Hellion on a sacrificial post," he began, rocking that child back and forth slowly.

"I knew the rules, but I could not leave her there to die. One thing led to another, I was attacked, and she saved me, claiming me to return the favor. It wasn't until forty-eight hours later that she and I became intimate. I do not know what she thinks of me, but I loved her and knew she left to protect us."

Selene looked towards Reid standing in the doorway, listening.

"If we ask for your help, will you come to our aid?" Selene asked, knowing Eddison had no idea Reid was there.

"I am the gatekeeper of Heaven, but Mora is mad with anger. She looks to Nova as if she is her own child. I was helpless to stop her from manipulating my child into taking that soul weapon."

"Did you try to break them apart?" Selene asked with no judgement.

He nodded, making sure to focus on the child in his arms.

"I hid who I was for over one-hundred-and-seventy-five years, but nothing I did stopped Nova's determination to become stronger. I couldn't hide who I was because of the guardian Angel but needed to stay there, for her."

"If we can guarantee your children will be free from Heaven and protected, will you help us?" Selene asked again.

Eddison looked over to her.

"Who is us? You are my sister, Selene, my family. I claim no side and my children are my priority."

Selene watched Reid leave the doorway out of the corner of her eye. This was the first step in ending this, ending the bloodshed and pain. People needed to be moved and those defenseless protected, but a few more needed rescuing. Reid was going to do that.

XXVII

"The Angels have advanced past our borders and will be at our main army in five hours," a soldier reported to Vadim.

"Number?" he signed.

"Five-hundred thousand. They are out for blood, with this base the center of their attack."

Vadim studied the map before him.

"Move the squads to the west to create a hole. We will draw them to the vantage point, so we have no more surprises. Is there anything else?" Vadim signed.

"Standard Angel guard, but one has a soul weapon and is showing no mercy."

Vadim looked up to the soldier who spoke in the crowded war room.

"All soul weapons are connected to the Heavenly king. Are you sure you have nothing to report about this Angelic soldier?" he signed.

All soldiers in the room fell silent. There was something else that they were too afraid to share. Before Vadim could demand an answer, Reid walked into the room.

Everyone bowed, including Vadim, to show respect.

"We will take over the initial attack. With the Angel wielding a soul weapon, the risk is too grand for a frontal assault," Reid signed the moment Vadim moved his head in his direction.

He didn't respond. Anger was obvious in Vadim's body language, but he was in no position to argue. No one could argue with Reid; he was the only one who had the ability to control the entire Hellion army, second to the king. His command was absolute.

*

Nova stood in the distance and listened to the conversations going on around her.

"We need to be careful. Multiple generals have been spotted in the area," an Angel reported.

Nova could not deny Mora's call. Even if her husband was the Dragon king, by accepting the sword to get stronger, she bound her body and soul to Mora. Her armor reflected Heaven, but her black wings isolated her from the others.

All soldiers avoided her, not only because of her nobility as the Dragon queen but due to how close she was to their king. No one befriended Mora, not in the way Nova had.

"We do not need your flashy sword. Stay in the back and out of our way," one of the Angels commanded.

All Nova wanted was to be strong. Her father and Kace were both strong, and she relied on their strength her entire childhood. But now, it was her turn to protect, to hold the strength when others could not.

"They took seventy percent of their squad and left the base camp. It is an opening we will take," the Angel announced.

Nova was not convinced it was a good plan. It would be a quick attack, but the generals were feared for a reason. This was a trap, but she would be ready.

When her feet touched the ground, there was no time to breathe. The eruption of bloodshed was instant. She took her first life and surprisingly, she felt no different. Each blade thrust caused her body to warm. Sweat fell from under her armor but if she slowed down, she would die.

"Die!" a Hellion soldier yelled.

Nova thrust her blade into its chest. The warm blood coated her armor, creating a numb feeling that overtook her. She had no words. Even if she could speak, there would be nothing to express about what her first battle made her feel.

Is this what it feels like to take a life? Empty? Nova had a loving husband, two beautiful boys, and she was happy. But this war, it took her mother, father, and her brother. It would take her boys, her husband, and she needed to protect them.

A figure in black appeared behind her and Nova didn't move fast enough. Her body felt his hand reaching through her blood-stained armor, and the black-cloaked figure disappeared only to reappear in the distance with Nova motionless over his shoulder and the soul weapon in his hand.

185

Only one person had the ability to touch a person's soul, and she was the one initiating the attack. By Reid not only being able to take it from Nova but also free her from its capture, he revealed a part of him he never wanted to admit. He looked at the battle around him and knew the woman he carried was now safe.

*

"Mommy?" Toer called out.

Nova stirred painfully but opened her eyes to look at the tear-stained cheeks of her firstborn. Her son was growing up and looking more and more like his father. When she was able to get her bearings, she realized he wasn't wearing any royal garments.

"I thought you were going to die," he said, and Nova's body screamed at her not to move.

"Ahh," she hissed and panicked when she heard her own voice.

"Toer, dear, your mother is fine," Selene said, walking into the room.

Nova recognized the smell of the coven; she had been here before. Her son did not fear the woman. He showed familiarity, which meant he had been here longer than Nova expected. Selene whispered something into Toer's ear that caused him to run out, then she sat down next to Nova, giving her a kind smile.

"Your wounds were severe. The armor did little to protect your body—"

"I shouldn't be able to speak," Nova said.

186

"Rather than focusing on that, let me tell you what that little boy has been through. He thought you were dead. Every day your husband brought him here to show that little boy you were alive and healing."

"I don't understand any of this . . ."

Nova only allowed one tear to escape, which Selene gently wiped away.

"Your father and I were born over two hundred years ago under the full moon. Our father was a gatekeeper, the last of his kind. It was his responsibility to keep his kind from going extinct. Do you know what you are, Nova, to Navar?" Selene asked.

Nova nodded.

"When I was two, I accidently opened a door to a world I didn't understand. The term gatekeeper wasn't a word I knew until I was older."

Selene gently took Nova's hand.

"Long ago, there was a key or gatekeeper for every world. A keeper to the king who ruled. That key was made for that person, to guide and educate. To be the conscience when they are confused and a lover if they needed."

"But there aren't any gatekeepers left . . .," Nova muttered.

"The former King of Heaven and Nobu, the current King of Hell, knew they were losing influence and control of their kings. They decided killing their kings would be the only way to guarantee control, but my father, your grandfather, escaped."

More tears escaped Nova's face when a wave of doubt and fear consumed her.

187

"Are you telling me my husband—"

Selene hit her on the back of the head.

"You are forgetting my children all have married their kings. Do not negate your husband's love for you. The world creates you for him, to love but never serve."

Nova rubbed her head and finally met Selene's gaze.

"My father is the gatekeeper of Heaven—"

Selene was starting to get annoyed with having to redirect Nova's thoughts.

"Your father and I mated for love. You and my children found love after duty. We failed, you did not."

"I do not know what to think about all of this, but I want to see my husband," Nova admitted, and Selene only nodded.

For four months Nova had been fighting to live, not only from her wounds but from the disconnection with the soul sword. It was the connection Reid severed that almost killed her, but it took away the hold and influence Mora had over Nova.

*

"You have wings like me!" Toer said when he walked over to Reid.

The little Dragon prince had been back and forth to the coven house for months, but this was his first-time seeing Reid. Never did Reid present himself as a general in his home. A simple pair of black pants and a shirt was all he needed. His white hair and red eyes were seen, but his wings were what got Toer all excited.

"Yes, little one, like you," Reid replied in a voice that reminded Eddison of Dinah.

"Are there more like me?" Toer asked, showing no fear towards Reid.

Eddison was frozen in the distance. This was a Hellion general. The instinct to grab his grandson and run was screaming at him, but Navar paced the room, showing no concern about the occupants. The soul sword Nova once possessed was near Reid, under his watchful eye.

"I have a sister and five brothers," Reid began, and Toer smiled ear to ear.

"Are there any kids?"

Reid chuckled. "I have six children, but I have a feeling there will be many more. You are never alone, young one, not anymore."

Navar and Eddison immediately looked at each other. A sister? Five brothers? There was no doubt in their minds that the information they learned (and assumed everyone whispered) was a fact. A fact that they quickly dismissed when a little girl Toer's age ran into the room.

"Grandpa!" she yelled and jumped into Reid's lap.

A smile crossed Reid's face at the small child. Her skin was the color of darkness with red-piercing eyes to show her Demonic side. Her tail wrapped around her leg, and the Demon princess hugged her grandfather tightly, happy to see him.

"How about you show your cousin around the ground while we wait for everyone else to show," Reid said, and the little girl named Maya grabbed Toer and dragged him out of the room.

Toer was not given a choice, but he did not argue. His eyes were glued to her wings that were like his. Raynar looked from his daughter to Navar and then to Eddison. No one had met the man, but there was no denying he was

189

Selene's twin. But when the second Dragon prince pulled on his leg trying to stand, Raynor didn't move.

Children did not judge based on appearance and were excellent judges of character. Keva wanted up, and the Demon king reached down and picked him up. When he pointed down the hallway, Raynar smiled and walked where he was commanded.

"You have rebelled," Eddison whispered to Navar.

"Do not misunderstand me, Eddison. Mora is a heartless wench who was going to sacrifice my wife. Her husband wasn't any better," Navar mumbled in response.

"I never doubted your intentions with Nova, not even when she was a child. You are honorable, and always did the right thing. Her happiness was all that mattered."

Navar listened to Eddison's words but watched as another child ran into the room.

"Excuse me!" that child yelled, running after Maya and Toer in the distance.

One looked to be a teenager with golden hair and pointed ears. Another child following close by seemed of Elven descent. The third boy in the group had see-through skin and similar features of the Spirit king. Children from rebellious realms.

"Generations fill these halls. It does not matter your origin or allegiance. Everyone is equal," Selene said, holding both of her sleeping infants.

Navar locked eyes with Nova, who walked behind Selene. She had tears falling down her face. Nova was scared and confused, but Navar moved quickly, holding her tightly in his arms. Nova was his everything and he almost lost her.

"I am sorry," Nova whispered, speaking the first words to her beloved since her vow of silence ten years ago.

"No, my love, I am sorry. I should have fought harder to include you, so you didn't feel alone."

190

Navar held her, knowing she needed to let the emotions take over before she could build herself back up.

Everyone gave their space to Navar and Nova. Malla walked up to her father, who was watching the children play in the garden outside.

"That is a new face," she commented, seeing the Dragon prince playing with her daughter.

"The Dragons have two sons," Reid said, pulling his daughter close.

"Heaven is advancing closer to Hell, and they are targeting the generals. I do not want you to fight," she whispered, holding onto her father tightly.

"I do not want you to worry about me or anything else. You and your family will be safe," Reid replied.

"We can help you, so you do not have to fight alone—"

Reid felt Selene walking up to him, and he gave his daughter a gentle kiss on the head, making sure she felt his strength.

"My main concern is this family's safety. Everything will fall into place," he said, and Malla nodded, joining her daughter outside a few moments later.

"They are all scared," Selene observed as Reid took his son Mica into his arms.

"Mora is out for blood, and with Nova no longer in her control, she will spiral," Reid observed and watched his son look around the room.

"Why?" Selene asked.

"Mora failed as a mother, and under the circumstances, she couldn't protect us from our father's wrath. Nova was her retribution and failed her too."

Selene held their other son safely in her arms.

"Did Mora make the connection that Nova belonged to Dinah?" she asked.

"What Mora went through over two hundred years ago broke her both mentally and physically. When Dinah released her into the world, she reclaimed Heaven and killed the former king. It was the downfall of any chance of happiness that woman would ever find. She doesn't have the ability to love those that were created out of hate."

Selene frowned.

"You need to talk to Dinah. She needs her family, regardless of the abuse she may have suffered. Her husband and children need her as much as I suspect she needs them."

Reid's mother was a secret no one knew. The seven Hellion generals only existed because of a deal made between Heaven and Hell. The two kings wanted the gatekeepers destroyed so they could rule. To gain entry to all the worlds, a child was created using the blood of both worlds. The queen was given to Hell by force, and as a result, Reid was created. Ripped from his mother's arms moments after his birth to train, to hunt, and to kill the gatekeepers, and he almost succeeded, until he met Selene.

"She is in Fae with her son," Reid finally said.

There was only supposed to be one general in existence. Reid was created for a purpose, and when he met and protected Selene, he found a purpose and a love he never felt before. One that ultimately made him the first of the generals to rebel.

"What is going on in that head of yours?" Selene asked.

"I am going to need all my brothers if we are going to survive. That will take time and we were raised to be obedient."

"Dinah and Qued are out of the king's graces, and from what you have told me about Vadim—about him taking care of Kace—I know he will help, if you ask."

Selene knew Reid would need to think about this more before he would act. She playfully spanked his butt before taking her son from his arms to put them both to bed. The first thing Reid needed to do was reunite mother and son, and he knew the Fae would not be receptive if he was the one who crossed into their territory.

XXVIII

Layla screamed the moment another contraction consumed her body.

"I want Kace!" she yelled, refusing to let anyone touch her.

Her water broke in the middle of the night, and the moment she started active labor, the doctor kicked Kace out of the room. It was not customary for the father to be in the room; men did not exist in Fae until Kace's soldiers showed up.

"You can't stop me," Kace threatened his mother, who was standing in front of his bedroom door.

Dinah had been in Fae in secret for four months. Not only has she gotten to know her son, but she helped train the soldiers in what to expect now that they were given free will. Six generals were now told Dinah was a traitor and would be hunting her, a number she didn't like now that her grandchild was coming into the world.

"I do not plan on it. No one was in the room when you and Nova were born. Your father delivered you," Dinah replied.

"So, if you are not going to stop me, why am I out here and not at my wife's side?" he asked angrily.

194

"Because you take after your father and follow the rules," she said, and Kace walked past her into the room.

Layla was surrounded by too many people. When her eyes found Kace, the pain on her face was gone, and she looked afraid. Before he could say anything, a familiar voice filled the room.

"How far along is she?" Eddison asked, creating a calm in the room.

"Both of you, out!" the doctor yelled as someone grabbed him from behind and forced him out of the room.

Layla had no idea what was going on, but when Eddison walked up to her, she saw a calm expression displayed on his face.

"My name is Dr. Eddison, and I am Kace's father."

In hearing that, Layla reached for Kace, and he was at her side in a heartbeat.

"Get it out," she demanded.

"The birth of a child is a powerful thing for both parents. It is wrong they forced you out, but it is up to your wife, if she will allow me to proceed," Eddison asked, and Layla only nodded, wanting this to be over.

The sound of Eddison's voice caused Dinah to flee. Eddison. She could not face him, but someone had grabbed her from behind and covered her mouth. When her wings went to defend, Reid pushed his body against hers. His eyes were hidden behind glasses as he looked at his sons. They both had been involved with the integration of the Dragons and their sisters' husbands' worlds. The Fae should be no different in agreeing to the alliance and the secrets they protect, but with Dinah here, things were a little more complicated.

Reid dragged her to the roof of the castle and finally let her go. She stumbled forward, but when Dinah turned to face her brother, she saw it was Reid. She was confused. Reid was the prodigy child, the strongest amongst them all, yet he was here when her grandchild was coming into this world.

"Dinah—" Reid said but she advanced, ready to attack.

She had speed but Reid was faster. He was always faster, and when Dinah's wings when to strike, he dodged. It was an ill attempt to try and fight him, but Reid never returned the attack.

"Dinah—" he tried to say but she was resistant to the sound of his voice and refused to allow him to harm her family.

"Stay away!" she snapped and grabbed his arm.

Reid got out of her hold and flipped her onto the ground. Arc and Ash pinned her down and made sure she was facing their father so a conversation could happen. Her eyes immediately went to the two redheaded twin boys and noticed that the uniforms, Siren, and Elf, were part of the rebellion.

"I am not here to hurt your family. All I need you to do is listen to me," he said as Dinah spread her wings, but Malla and Tallia appeared, pinning them down.

"I nor my children will hurt you, Dinah. Your son and his father will help the Fae bring that child into this world. It is you and me here," he said and removed her blindfold.

Slowly she opened her eyes and looked at her brother.

"Why?" she asked, tears falling down her face.

"I will not go back; I refuse to go back!" Dinah added while Reid took off his glasses, truly seeing his sister for the first time.

"No one will ever harm you again. I will protect you and yours. All I ask is for you to trust me," Reid nodded, and his children let her go.

Dinah did not hesitate. She sat up quickly and punched Reid hard in the face. He did not block the blow, but he did not move so Dinah would understand he was true to his word.

"You were there when our father beat me, tortured me. He dragged me around by my hair like I was a doll. You did nothing! Trust you? I despise you!" she yelled and stood.

Reid did not move as she walked away, all he did was watch the blood drip from his broken nose. Gold. Royal blood ran through his veins, and everything she accused him of was correct. He did nothing to stop him.

"Father?" Tallia asked, not knowing what to do.

"I need a count of all the individuals and soldiers in this realm. Once completed, I want the four of you to go back to the house," he commanded, and they knew better than to argue.

*

"Are you alright?" Layla asked.

A few hours ago, she brought the first male born into the world of Fae since the curse was cast. Thousands of years only females walked this realm. It was a long and painful process, one that she would remember if the talk of having children came up again. When Eddison approached the bed, he handed the crown prince to her.

"Ten fingers and ten toes. Perfectly healthy," Eddison reported.

Kace could not look away from his son. A boy, his child. He was perfect, but the fear of something being wrong was still there. Fae women did not birth boys, which was the curse set by Nobu. But here he was, his child, his son, one that he would do everything in his power to protect.

Eddison did not want to disturb the moment. He slowly walked out of the room, but Kace quickly followed. Ten years. It had been ten years since he had seen him, and Kace would admit that he missed him. Eddison knew Kace would follow, and when he did, he grabbed his son and brought him close. Even though they now look eye to eye, he was still his baby boy.

"I am so proud of you, Kace," Eddison whispered.

"I tried to find you, to save you," Kace began, and Eddison held onto him harder.

"It isn't your job to protect me. I am the one who should be sorry."

Kace never let emotions overtake him—it was how he survived—but the tears would not stop. This man was his everything, the only kind hand he ever knew, and upon hearing his father's voice, the shield he spent ten years building broke.

The attack on the hospital played in Kace's mind repeatedly. He was weak back then, but now, he could protect his family. It took him a long time to be able to let his father go, and when he returned to his room, he found his wife and child in a place he never wanted to leave.

"Kace?" Layla asked, watching him closely.

"Hm?"

Layla watched Kace focus all his attention on their sleeping son, as if he was going to disappear if he looked away.

"You haven't talked about the fact that both of your parents are here."

He shrugged.

"What do you want me to say?"

Layla got closer to him.

"Your father got into my world without permission, like your mother, in time to help us bring our son into this world. They both do what they please without any regard to the rules. Why haven't you talked to them? Or reintroduced them to each other? It has been what, thirty years?"

Layla never pushed herself into Kace's personal life, but this was different. All he ever wanted was his family, his parents, but he feared that they would disappear again.

"It isn't that simple . . .," he muttered.

"The past is the past, Kace. Our son is here and needs his father. I cannot lose you to this war, which is why I am going to officially join the rebellion and help put a stop to this needless bloodshed."

When their son Cameron cried, Layla picked him up. Her magic may have healed her body, but the need to take it easy was ordered by Eddison. She needed to bond with her son and realize that the world would get a lot more complicated now that there was a child involved.

*

"General. A representative is here for you," a soldier reported when he found Kace walking the halls a few hours later.

"From?" he inquired.

"The Dragon realm, but forgive me, general, I cannot repeat the words she expressed towards you."

Kace sighed loudly, knowing exactly who was calling.

"Is it a redhead that has my face but is female?"

The soldier nodded.

Had it really been ten years since he had seen Nova? The soldier informed him that his sister was in the drawing room, and Kace walked slowly towards that location. The night their seals were broken, and their wings were awakened was the only time he ever broke a promise to his sister. He promised to protect her, but he left her like their mother did, and he knew she wasn't going to forgive him so easily.

"She is going to kill you," Navar said when he saw Kace approach the door.

Kace looked at the Dragon king and questioned how he could be here. Navar smirked at Kace's confusion, and when he walked over to his wife's brother, he placed a hand on his shoulder.

"Don't worry. A lot has happened for the both of you. I am sure the beating will be short lived, but do not let her go too far, she is still healing," Navar explained and walked away.

Kace slowly reached for the door and opened it. There was no point in avoiding what was about to happen. When he saw his sister, she was exactly how he remembered her. Rageful and beautiful, no longer did she wear the long flowing dresses; it was all tactical. The bandages he could see from her low-cut shirt showed the golden stains of their blood, along with fading scars of battle.

"I thought I was the only one with battle scars," Kace teased but ducked when a book flew in his direction.

With every step Nova took towards him, Kace noticed a limp. Her arms held muscles and scars. Her whole body was molded into that of a soldier, and he could only frown. He never wanted this life for her.

"Nova—"

"You left me!" she yelled and punched Kace hard across the face.

Another punch landed moments later. Every time she took a swing, Kace didn't block it. Even when her stitches started to rip, he let her get it all out. Dinah slowly walked closer to her children with a frown on her face.

Kace. He'd aligned himself with Fae, and her daughter, her beautiful vibrant child was a casualty of war. Nova's wings were folded behind her back, and when she swung again, Dinah reached forward and stopped it. This was not the first time she had to stop a fight, and Reid wasn't the only one who knew how to subdue an individual with black wings.

Dinah wrapped one arm around her daughter's waist and pressed her body against Nova. If her child chose to sharpen them it would hurt, but Nova went willingly, as if knowing who was holding her.

"Shhh," Dinah whispered, and Nova screamed.

The screams were filled with pain and loneliness. Hatred and fear. She was alone, always had been because the one she always trusted to have her back left her all those years ago. Eddison listened on the other side of the door and heard a voice that he knew from his dreams. He wanted to run into that room and hold the woman he loved, but for now, their daughter needed her more than he did.

XXIX

"Where is he?" Nova grumbled when she awoke four days later.

The coven house had been a neutral place for everyone to gather. Nova knew she overdid it, but when she saw her brother, she was so angry. That anger turned to rage, and all she wanted to do was beat him until he was within an inch of his life so he could feel an ounce of what she felt being left behind.

"It has been four days. I do not like the idea of you beating him up at the expense of reinjuring yourself," Navar replied.

For him to be here meant her children were here too. But when she didn't hear them, she started to get worried.

"The boys?"

Navar took a moment to answer, but when he did, that rage returned.

"Layla is watching them."

"Why is the Fae king watching our sons?" she snapped.

Navar reached forward, moving some hair out of her face.

"Your brother is the gatekeeper to the Fae and wanted to meet his nephews—"

"That doesn't excuse that lying sack of shit! I am going to kill him!" she announced and tried to stand.

Navar pulled her into his embrace, making sure to be mindful of her injuries.

"I love you," Navar whispered into her ear.

Tears threatened to fall but she refused to give in to the complex emotions she was feeling. She could listen to Navar talk about gatekeepers and kings. She didn't care about the rebellion. All Nova wanted was her family safe—all but her brother. He needed to be hurt.

Navar carefully let her go, and she was out the door faster than he expected. The voices in the distance were mixed, but she knew her brother was amongst them; she could hear that bastard. When she barged through the open doorway, Eddison was there immediately to catch her.

"Let me go!" Nova yelled.

"Enough!" Eddison yelled back.

Kace couldn't help but feed into the madness. He walked over and carefully poked her face, making sure he was far enough out of reach.

"To be young again . . ." Tallia smirked and looked at her husband, who didn't show the same enthusiasm.

"They are only twenty years younger than you," her brother, Arc, informed.

"Mother said you and Ash used to fight nonstop until you had better influence."

The noise the trio was making caught everyone's attention, including Selene who was sitting in Reid's lap, enjoying the peaceful moment.

"You going to break it up?" Selene asked Reid.

"Not my children. Dinah can handle them," he replied and looked up to the second-floor balcony where Dinah was slowly pacing.

Everyone knew Dinah was angry but not why. Kace did not fight back when Nova got out of her father's hold and pinned her brother to the floor. It was Layla who was the levelheaded one of the group.

"Kace!"

Kace immediately flipped Nova off him and joined his wife's side. There was a bond that everyone seemed to have with their partner, and when Raynar, the Demon king, looked at Layla, he had a mischievous look on his face.

"I missed your temper, Layla—"

"Hell lost its strongest magical ally," Cain, the Spirit king, added, enjoying the commotion around him.

"Shove it, both of you!" Layla snapped.

"Heaven is attacking all general camps. It isn't random," Willow, the Elven king, muttered to the group around her.

When Reid slowly stood, everyone looked at him. Eddison was the only one in the room who was still uncomfortable with the sight of another Hellion general, but when he kept his eyes on Dinah, everyone started to give their input.

"All generals have been spotted in the Mortal realm, and Heaven is the front of every attack. No place is safe," Malla added.

"She won't stop," Nova muttered, slowly getting up off the floor.

Reid held out his hand, and a sword appeared, Nova's sword. When he threw it up, everyone watched Dinah reach out for it, catching it. Arc and Ash rushed to their wives while Malla and Tallia went for their children, but Reid raised his hand and every door in the room slammed shut, locking them in.

"Between my children's armies and my own, I can protect all rebelled realms, but I cannot fight against her alone. I am not asking for forgiveness, Dinah, I do not deserve it, but your children need protection. Will you help?" Reid called out.

To be able to hold a holy weapon, a soul blade, you needed the blood of the creator and their strength. Only seven people existed that could hold this blade without a vow, and two were in this room.

"I have no army," Dinah replied and looked at Kace.

"But you have the knowledge to make sure we all survive," Reid replied.

Dinah dropped the blade and it vanished, gone back to the nothingness it was created from.

"We have three generals. If we get Vadim and Qued on our side, we may stand a chance," she said and walked out of the room with Eddison running after her.

"You're letting him go but not us?" Arc asked his father, but Reid focused on Kace.

"Vadim won't trust me."

Kace shrugged. "You're the boogeyman. They fear you. But I do not trust Vadim or Qued around my family. If you include them, you will lose the Fae support."

206

The way Kace spoke to him, it was with a level of respect a soldier gave to another. It wasn't how he talked but also how he moved. Raynar smiled, finally understanding who was underneath the Fae clothing before them.

"You risky little minx, you snagged yourself a general," Raynar whispered to Layla who rolled her eyes.

"Are you telling me Kace is the rising eighth general? The one behind the mask?" Malla asked, now with a hundred questions running through her mind.

*

Eddison heard the commotion, knew that something was going to happen, but he had to see her. Had to hold her. He was tired of running, of fearing that what they had wasn't real. When he finally found Dinah, she had her back to him.

"Dinah—"

"I can't, Eddison," she whispered.

He took another step forward, reaching out for her. When Dinah felt his arms around her, tears started to fall. She wasn't weak, but she hated these feelings that were inside her. Dinah wanted to fight, wanted to run away— but to feel him, smell him, she needed that too.

"I am not letting you go, Dinah. I was foolish the first time but not this time . . ."

Dinah didn't reply. Like her daughter, she needed to get the emotions out.

*

While Eddison and Dinah were finally reuniting, Kace found his infant son and carefully returned him to his mother so he could be fed.

"I will help under one condition," Kace said, knowing that Layla would give him an earful after making the entire room wait thirty minutes for him to change his mind.

"Which is?" Reid asked.

"Follow me . . .," Kace muttered, and Reid obeyed.

No one commanded Reid, especially in his own house, but the general knew he needed Kace to win this war. Something was happening, a shift that everyone could feel. Even though Reid did all he could to protect his family, the increase of rebellious races hadn't gone unnoticed.

XXX

Nobu was furious. The Angels' attacks were solely against the generals' camps, leaving everyone else alone. It was deliberate, and it confused him because by Mora attacking the generals, she was attacking her own children. He thought Heavenly beings had love and attachment to those they birthed.

"Tell me where they are . . .," he growled to everyone in the room.

"We have one in custody while the others are in the Mortal world. The one you inquire about cannot be found," a minion replied.

The king needed to find him, the one they called Reid. Names. He didn't care what they called themselves, they were a body that would obey. The images of the never-ending battle scenes added to his anger; he needed to step away to control himself.

The generals were fighting to survive, at least the ones he could find. When Nobu entered a room, a man stood there. His hair was white like the generals and his eyes glistened a deep red. Wings of darkness were nestled gently on his back, but his face was the reason no one knew he existed. This man shared the same face as Reid.

"Father," the man said and bowed.

209

"Something is happening, and I need you to find out what. Give me a report on all the generals and if you find *him,* bring that disappointment to me."

The king trusted no one, not even his own children, but that man, Reid's twin, was the exception. Separated at birth, he wasn't trained to be a warrior but an assassin. His body was lean over built, fast over sturdy. Only one child had the privilege of calling him father, and that child would fix everything.

*

An infant crying in the distance caused Vadim to stir. His mind was groggy, and his body was in severe pain. Every second for the past week he had been fighting. Countless victories were won but that didn't negate the general from injury.

"Look who finally woke up," Layla said, slowly walking around the room.

Upon hearing the voice, Vadim opened his eyes. He panicked. The blind wasn't across his face, and his red-jeweled eyes found the Fae king walking around the room. She had an infant in her arms, the one that he read about in Kace's letter, but Vadim should be on the battlefield, not here. When he tried to move, his whole body hurt.

"Your wings were damaged and are now bound. For them to heal, it would be wise not to use them. Kace told me not to use Fae magic to heal you out of fear of rejection. If you are to stay in my home, Vadim, I expect you to be an asset over a problem."

210

Vadim blinked once more and focused on the child in her arms. Its wings were slowly growing its feathers, but he seemed uncomfortable, which Layla noticed as well. Vadim should be anxious, fighting to get back out to the battlefield, but he felt calm, almost content, with being taken care of for the first time.

"Your mouthpiece was removed when Kace brought you in. You are welcome to use sign language, but I suggest using the voice you were refused all your life," Layla informed and walked out of the room to address her child.

She spoke sweet words to that baby. When she closed the door, Kace leaned up against the wall. He stood there, looking to Vadim with an expression the man couldn't read. There was no pity or sadness, but Vadim raised his bandaged hands to talk because he was too afraid to use his voice.

"Why am I here?" Vadim signed.

"Injuries will do that to a man," Kace teased.

"Don't be fresh. I cannot be here, Kace. Layla rebelled. I have orders to kill her on sight,"

Vadim replied but flinched when his hands started to hurt.

Kace smirked. "But you won't."

Vadim raised an eyebrow, and Kace threw a robe to him, making his intentions known that they were going to be walking. Vadim had known the kid for over ten years. He was a good soldier but an arrogant man. Humor and friendship could get a person killed, but Vadim refused to let that happen.

When they both slowly walked down the hall, Vadim didn't say anything. He was in hiding, no one knew he was here, he had a feeling Kace had something to ask.

"You lost fifteen percent of your total army with over sixty injured. We were able to bring them here to recover, but they will await your command when you are ready."

Both men looked out the window when Kace finished. Each soldier created for a general was a shell, a body stolen from a mortal and transformed. Each carried the king's seal, so when Vadim saw Kace's soldiers carrying the seal of the Fae, he looked at him.

"Free will?" he struggled to say, using his voice for the first time.

Kace nodded. "For the past year they were all given free will and a choice. They were to either live the rest of their lives as a civilian or continue to serve as a soldier. Many chose to stay with what they knew, but a few settled down and found a life for themselves, one they were robbed of when Nobu stole their bodies."

"I can't be here, Kace—"

Kace didn't let him finish.

"You were there for me, helped protect me when I was lost. It is my turn now, Uncle."

Uncle. To hear Kace say those words meant he knew the truth, and when the panic crossed his face, Dinah appeared and pulled Vadim away from her son.

"You should be resting . . .," she growled.

Dinah gave Vadim no choice, she dragged him back into the room and threw him on the bed. It was true, Vadim needed to heal, but Dinah also didn't trust him to walk around the castle. He was Kace's responsibility, and when they were alone, Vadim looked over to his nephew.

"How did you know I was your uncle?" he asked.

The shock of being here was gone; it had been a few hours since he awoke. When he looked at Kace for an answer, the man smirked.

"Process of elimination. Same facial features and characteristics," he began and handed Vadim a cup of water.

"And I asked," Kace added and winked.

"You're lying—"

"When you have a child, the world becomes a scary place. I couldn't let you die, you're the only one that knows that part of my life and understands what I am. I know the king will put a bounty on your head when you are reported missing, but I need you. I know it sounds selfish, but I can't let you die for a man who uses his own children as pawns."

Vadim didn't know what to say to that. He had time to process what was happening, but he couldn't understand why Kace was doing this. When he didn't respond, Kace knew he wanted to be left alone. But after he walked out of the room, Dinah stepped out, furious.

"That boy looks to you as a hero, a man with all the answers, but you and I both know that you are nothing more than a pound of flesh at our father's disposal," she growled.

Vadim had no more fight left in him. When he looked at his sister, he could see her not as the woman before him, but as the helpless victim of their king, who took out all

213

his anger on her. He couldn't shake the guilt but knew there was nothing he could do.

"What that man did to you was deplorable, but your own vile hatred—"

"Idiot," Dinah began.

"This isn't about me, and you know it. I could have fought back, but if I did, he would have known I had something to live for. It was a sacrifice any mother would make for her child."

"Qued sacrificed himself to rescue you, and now is in and out of cells to keep Nobu's eyes off of you," Vadim began, emotion finally showing.

"We can feel, Dinah. The longer we are exposed to the emotions of this world, the easier it makes it for us to understand. Your son showed me how to feel, and when he rebelled, it felt like I lost a child—"

Dinah was ready to fight. "He is my son, not yours!"

*

The sounds coming out of that room were heard throughout the castle. Eddison and Kace flinched when something shattered and ripped. Sometimes people needed to talk it out, others needed to use a more physical approach.

"Do you think Mother will kill him?" Kace asked his father, concerned.

"Maybe," Eddison muttered and watched Dinah limp out of the room.

"He is in," she snapped, slowly walking away.

214

"The Hellion city you and your sister grew up in was hers before you took over. Your mother will always be more terrifying than you could ever be," Eddison said and followed his wife, knowing that Kace will take care of the general who now was part of the rebellion.

XXXI

"The letter from Kace explains that Vadim is adjusting nicely to Fae, and Dinah is working with both armies. It was easier than you thought," Selene announced as she watched her husband pace around the garden.

It was a beautiful day, and it was the two of them with their infant sons rolling around on a blanket. Times like these were rare, when Reid was able to spend time with his wife without the presence of another, but the thought of what was happening dampened what would have been a good afternoon.

"Vadim thinks Layla and Kace are going in alone. He will protect his ward, but that doesn't mean he will help me protect my family," Reid observed.

"What about Qued?" Selene asked.

"That man was never able to stay still: he broke out of yet another cell, and I am waiting to hear back from Ash and Arc about his current location."

When Selene reached for his pant leg, Reid stopped pacing. When he looked down to his wife, she pulled his leg out from under him and watched him fall. Selene slowly climbed upon him and looked into his beautiful eyes.

"You listen to me carefully. Everything happens for a reason, my love. The good and the bad. It shapes who we are, and I will not let you take the weight of everyone's problems on your shoulders," she said and kissed him gently.

Reid only smiled at her tender touch, but when their sons started to fuss, Selene's attention was diverted. Small moments were what kept a person whole. They were what was held in the darkest of times, to keep one sane and alive.

When Reid looked up to the sky, he thought he saw a bird, but it was moving too fast towards him to be an animal.

These mountains were protected by the coven. His soldiers guarded what the magic could not keep out, but Reid did not sense the individual who appeared on top of him with a sword aimed for his chest.

His face and body were covered, and those black wings helped the masked man stay on Reid's chest weightlessly, but Reid caught the blade right before it plunged deep into his body. All seven generals were accounted for, so who was this man?

"Found you," the masked assailant whispered and dropped the sword only to draw a dagger.

His speed was something Reid had never seen before. Reid was always the fastest and strongest, but this man was faster. When Reid tried to get up, to move, he felt a blade pierce his back where the man appeared. Another pierced his side, and then his front. He was moving too fast for Reid to track.

Reid's eyes locked on Selene, who was watching in horror from a distance. She could not be caught. When the masked individual threw a blade towards Selene, Reid moved with the last ounce of his strength in front of her and caught it with his body.

"Run," he managed to say before the sword was plunged deep into his chest.

It happened in an instant. Too fast for Reid to think. He was never outwitted, outsourced, and overpowered, so this was the first time he felt completely helpless.

*

Layla appeared in the coven house the moment a messenger reached her realm. This could not be right, Reid could not have been taken, and when she opened every door of the home, she could not find Selene either.

"Where are the babies?" she yelled at the terrified Witches around her.

Two crying baby boys were brought to her, without their mother around to protect them. The messenger was a failsafe if something were to ever happen to Reid. It was strange that the general would trust his soldiers, his family, in Layla's hands, but it made sense. Layla married the rising eighth general, and his mother and Vadim were with him. They were to handle his soldiers, and she was to handle the rest.

"Send word to Selene's children. They are to come here, but do not tell them what has happened," she ordered.

*

"Where are we?" Vadim asked as he and Dinah stood on the balcony watching Layla maintain control.

"There was a reason Reid was always distant with us," Dinah muttered.

Navar and Nova were the next ones to enter the coven house. Layla was strategic. The generals' armies would cover the ground, but she needed someone to cover the sky. It was an attack, there wasn't another word for what happened.

Then Qued appeared behind Dinah and Vadim; he looked a little beaten up.

"I have been dodging a lifetime of imprisonment, and you two look like you've been to a party."

Qued was grumpy, but when he joined his brother and sister, he looked at the chaos below. Moving pieces to protect, detect, and prevent. No one looked up, they were all looking at what was before him.

Kace watched the three generals observe, and for the first time, they were still.

"You do not seem conflicted about what is unfolding," Vadim said to Qued.

To see another general without a mouthpiece and uniform was a comfort, but it also felt different. Qued only shrugged. He was officially on the run, and no longer needed to be under someone's direction. It was freeing.

"I sealed my fate by releasing Dinah. Father never saw us as anything other than pawns, and Mother hated us on sight."

The green grass outside the windows was immediately covered in armies. Soldiers serving their kings proudly stood side by side with those who joined their cause. Spirits, Demons, Sirens, and Elves: all members of the rebellion followed the call and came when the one man that bound them together was taken.

"We have the entire rebellion at our feet," Vadim stated.

"What is the emergency?" Arc demanded as the four siblings approached Navar.

Layla held no emotion on her face. "Your father was attacked, and, in the process, both of your parents were taken. We do not have enough information to know where they were taken, but the coven and your brothers are safe—"

"What do you mean taken?" Tallia snapped.

"How do you know this and not us?" Malla, her sister, yelled.

Layla raised her hands to stop the siblings from talking over each other.

"I received a message from your father's command. Once I arrived, we found signs of a struggle in the garden. Reid's soldiers swept the area, and with the Dragons in the sky, there is no opening for a second attack. I need the four of you to think logically and help me find them."

"So, the twin thing isn't an accident. You are the gatekeeper of the Fae, your sister the Dragon. Am I to assume the two pairs of redheaded twins are the keys to the colors they wear?" Vadim asked Kace.

Kace couldn't answer because the screaming below increased.

"It must be a general! They are the only people who could have tracked his movements," Ash stated.

"He gives us too much credit," Qued muttered.

"It is not a general," Nova said, trying to help her sister-in-law calm the gatekeepers down.

"How could you possibly know that? Your mother was imprisoned for your entire life! You haven't been around them long enough to understand!" Arc yelled.

"Did you take Reid?" Nova yelled, but before Ash could demand her silence, all the generals looking from the balcony above responded.

"No."

Everyone turned and looked up. Two faces were familiar, but the other two caused a raise of alarm. They went to attack, and Layla and Nova tried to calm them down.

"Reid is the father, isn't he?" Vadim asked, and their conversation now had an audience.

"Yes," Kace replied.

"The mother?" Qued asked.

"My husband's twin sister," Dinah answered.

"I do not have to take orders from you!" Arc yelled towards them, and Kace smirked.

"To find a general, you need a general. I have four. How many do you have?" Layla challenged the group in front of her.

"I will assess the situation and report back," Vadim said and vanished.

221

"I have a few contacts I can use," Qued added and disappeared as well.

Reid's children were scared. They grew up with both parents and built a solid foundation based on family. Nova and Kace didn't have the strong familial connection, but Kace trusted his mother to watch over the coven as he went to aid in the search for Reid. One general controlled the entire outcome, and it wasn't Dinah. It was Reid, and if something happened to him, the entire rebellion would fall apart.

XXXII

"Father," the man who the king called Zero stated, bowing before the King of Hell.

"Did you find *him?*" Nobu asked.

"Detained and immobile," Zero replied.

"Good. Keep him there until I fix this rising rebellion."

Zero watched the king observe the images in the sphere and give commands. Secrets surrounded the king. It brought his children together over apart. Reid was bound, gagged, and unconscious. It must remain that way to prevent him from escaping. The cells were not meant to hold Hell's brilliant creations. If Reid had indeed gone against Nobu, the king could not let him live.

*

"Are you still sleeping?" a small child asked Selene.

Her head was throbbing, and her body was sore. What had happened in the garden came back in flashes. Reid. Her babies. It was a warm day that turned dark when that man came from the sky. Selene opened her eyes and looked at the red-jeweled eyes of that child.

Red eyes, grey skin, and elongated canine teeth. Vampire. Yet, the way this child was looking to Selene wasn't hostile, but playful.

"See! I told Daddy that you were awake!" she said all excited.

She vanished instantly. Vampires could not use magic, but they could control the space around them and move fast enough to seem like they vanished. Selene did catch a glimpse of that small girl's back. Black wings.

Selene pushed the covers away and fell flat on her face. Images of her husband being attacked and her boys screaming filled her thoughts. Her babies. She had to make sure they were alright, but when she tried to get up again, she felt a weight on her leg.

A golden chain was tied to the bedpost. It glistened when she moved it. The incantations on the metals suppressed her magic, and she felt the drain in her power. A door opened in the distance and a few female Vampires came into the room.

Vampires were not part of the rebellion. They spoke in a language she did not know and presented her with clothing to change into. She feared the pain they would inflict on her, but instead, they tended to her wounds, washed her face, and helped her dress.

If Selene fought them, she would be killed. She had to endure. That little girl ran into the room, excited, and reached for Selene's hand.

"Are you ready?" she asked.

Selene only nodded, not knowing what to say. That child's hand was warm over cold. When the girl dragged her forward, the chain turned to an anklet, and Selene could follow her lead. The child was happy, excited even in the presence of a stranger. Her red dress matched Selene's new clothing; it was assumed this was the color of this realm.

"Daddy told me you may not know the Vampire language so it would be best to speak this mortal one. I know many languages, do you?" she asked.

Those eyes looked back to Selene when she was dragged into a drawing room. Those big, dark-ruby eyes were filled with curiosity over fear. Guards were on either side of the wall, watching them, waiting for Selene to make a mistake. It was a test to see if trust could be gained.

"How many?" she asked again.

"A few dozen . . .," Selene muttered, taking in the large room.

"Whoa! My name is Faith. I should have introduced myself sooner, shoot," the girl said and let Selene's hand go, running deeper into the room.

"As long as you play along and keep that smile on the little girl's face, all will be well," a female voice said behind Selene.

When Selene looked behind her, the woman's face was hidden underneath a giant hood. The feeling she gave was eerie, almost like death. Selene refused to speak, refused to be afraid, even though her body was trembling.

"Ibitzee!" the child yelled and ran into the arms of the cloaked figure.

The body language of that figure changed from hostile to friendly. Not much was seen, but that little girl held onto her with familiarity and a smile.

"Are you taking good care of Miss Selene? Cousin William asked me to help you. What would you like me to do?" the woman asked, and the child started talking too fast for Selene to keep up.

A Vampire and Death. Selene needed to get out of this room. Reid. Her babies. She needed to find them. The Vampires were a Hellion race, and they were aligned with the Hellion king. Nobu would kill Selene on sight if she was ever found.

"Tea! I will go and get you some!" Faith announced and ran out of the room.

"You are such a liar. You wanted to see Selene as much as I did," a male voice said from across the room.

Two clothed figures now looked towards Selene. Both held the familiar feeling of death and dread. But a third voice caused Selene to slowly back towards an open door leading to a balcony.

"You both are in so much trouble," a new woman said.

This third person caused Selene to take another cautious step backwards. Black wings and red hair tied back in a dark chain. Her eyes were jeweled, like Selene's children, but they were brown, not purple. Something was wrong.

"Speak for yourself. If your brother finds you out here, he will tell your father," Ibitzee stated.

Faith entered the room with a tray in hand. That happy expression changed when she saw the two newcomers. A temper was starting to rise in that little girl, but before she could spew the nastiness bubbling, a fourth figure entered the room.

"Now Faith, we need to stay calm," the new individual warned, and his face matched the woman with the red hair.

Twins. Red hair. Black wings. It was too much of a coincidence not to be a problem. Only she and Eddison had the ability to create gatekeepers, and these were not her children, nor were they her brothers.

"I am sorry you were introduced to us this way, Selene. We all know of you and were excited to be able to finally meet you. I am William, and the woman you are looking to is my sister Katarina."

"I am in Hell. It isn't safe," Selene whispered and took another step back.

"Yes, you are in Hell, but this is my home, Selene, you are safe—"

"I don't even know you!" Selene called out, taking another step backwards.

"I—"

"Release me from my bind! I need to find my husband and children!"

The man known as William shook his head. "I am unable to fulfill your request. That bind is not only restricting your magic, but it is preventing the Hellion King Nobu from sensing your presence."

Reid. Her babies. Her family. She couldn't be here, she needed to find them. With all the courage she had left in her body, Selene turned and ran for the balcony. Before

227

anyone in the room could reach her, she jumped over the railing and down to the ground below.

Selene landed in a bush to break her fall, but she was only able to gain two steps before she was punched in the face, causing her to fall onto her back.

"There is no easy way to transition you into this, so I am going to say it," a new face said and looked down at Selene.

"You were brought here instead of Nobu's castle. We could have let you rot and be tortured like your husband is now, but I have a soft spot for you, my sister. But that familial relation you and I share will quickly disappear if you disrespect me or my family again."

That man looked so much like her father. Dark eyes and red hair. There were subtle differences, but there was no mistaking he was her father's son. It never occurred to Selene that there might be more gatekeepers, but the fear from seeing the man didn't waver because she was now in Hell and at his mercy.

XXXIII

The five rebellious kings gathered in the coven house. There was little time when they were alone to talk, but at this moment, a conversation needed to happen so everyone was on the same page.

"Why was the messenger sent to you?" the Siren King Morgaine asked.

"Because…," Layla muttered in response, looking over the map of the Hellion territories.

"Your general broke your curse—" Raynar started.

"If any of you have something to say, say it," she snapped.

The Spirit King Cain spoke first.

"Your general's loyalty is to you and only you. We all have our spouses half the time because of their connection to their parents but not you . . ."

"The generals were created for war; they would have lost their purpose if there was a victor," Willow, the Elven king added.

Dinah watched over everyone at the coven but was growing impatient. Vadim. Qued. Kace. They were using their resources, but now a connection was being formed between them. Even if they didn't fully trust each other, a weakness was gained when allies formed.

Navar had walked away from the conversation when he spotted Dinah up above. He never had a chance to talk to the mother of his wife, but when he walked closer, he stopped.

"I am not going to bite," Dinah grumbled in agitation.

"I have no objection to my wife having a relation with you general, but you and I—"

Dinah knew what he was going to say but she gathered her courage and faced the Dragon king.

"I never wanted this for my children. I sacrificed my life so they could have a clean start. Layla's job is to keep the families in line—"

"I do not need a keeper," Navar growled, easily distracted by her taunts.

It was hard for Dinah to ask for help or rely on others. Eddison had been at her side for weeks, helping her through the nightmares and feelings of hopelessness, but his sister was missing, and he needed to find her.

"I need you to watch over the kings and their families, and keep your wife out of Heaven," Dinah said and Navar frowned.

"If you do this, you could die," he replied, knowing what she had planned.

"My children lived for thirty years without me: they will be fine in my absence," she said and vanished, going after the one woman who was the key in ending the bloodshed.

*

Heaven was a place of purity and grace. Less than thirty races now followed and supported Mora, and since Navar's rebellion, she locked every portal out of the Heavens. Mora would never admit that her defenses were weakened when Navar left. So, when Dinah appeared in the hallway, the general took a deep breath.

The soul sword she had within her gave her the key to break the barriers. Part of her felt calm in being here, but the Hellion side felt the pain in every breath she took. It was one of the reasons their father forced them to wear a mask: to hide their voice and not let their Hellion side show weakness.

"Excuse me," a servant said.

Dinah spread her wings wide. Her white hair flew in the wind they created. She needed to be seen, for Mora to know she was here, and when the guards hesitated to approach her, she knew what to do.

"Get me Mora or I will find her myself!" Dinah yelled.

The pain in her life started when Dinah felt empathy towards the woman who bore her. It didn't take long, only moments for Mora to feel her power, but at first glance, she mistook her for the one person Dinah refused to allow to be used ever again.

"Nova?" Mora called out, but her face changed when she saw her own daughter's face.

"Hello, Mother," Dinah said.

"Dinah—"

231

"The fight between you and me is here. Where is Reid?" she demanded.

Spikes appeared on the ground and Mora took a step back. When Dinah went to advance, Eddison appeared and wrapped his arm around Dinah's waist. Her portals may have been closed, and Dinah may have snuck in with the soul sword, but Eddison didn't need to knock. How protectively he held onto Dinah caused Mora to frown.

"I do not know who you speak of, Dinah. You nor your brothers should have been able to remove Nova's—" Mora stopped when she realized what Dinah said.

"Where is Reid?"

"My mother suffered over thirty years of abuse because she helped you escape. You didn't save her," Kace began behind Mora as the entire hallway filled with his soldiers.

"You took my vulnerable sister and made her a tool in your game for revenge."

Mora looked towards the voice and saw Nova's face. Twins. She forgot the fact all gatekeepers came in pairs. Nova was her focus, which hid Kace from Mora's detection. Then she saw the Fae symbol on Kace's armor and scowled.

"If we fight, your family will die," Mora said, knowing that the Fae king had a son not too long ago.

"Good thing he is not alone," Tallia said, and the twins appeared beside Kace.

Siren. Elf. Demon. Spirit. Four races of the rebellion flooded the halls and outside the castle. It was an invasion, one that Mora did not foresee.

"You spread your army too thin amongst the Mortal realms. You left little to defend you and your home. Those who rebelled against you were locked out, even your own gatekeeper, but here they are, taking down the one who betrayed them," Raynar said from the darkness that surrounded them.

"You do not know what Nobu did to me. How he forced me to bear his children, then ripped them from my arms. In their faces . . . all I see is him!" Mora yelled, but when she went to attack, two strong sets of arms grabbed her from behind.

Kelby. Everard. They held onto their mother tightly as she flailed and screamed. Power. When she tried to use it, nothing happened. The power of the King of Heavens was granted to the one with unimaginable strength, but once that power was lost, the wings turned back to white. Mora no longer held that power, and as she kicked and cried, she showed her children that she was nothing more than a victim of war.

"She stopped being a king the moment she cast her armies into the Mortal realm and killed millions of innocent mortals. They looked to us for protection, a symbol of balance and peace, but now they fear us like the Hellions," Malcom said and watched Kelby knock his mother unconscious to stop the screaming.

XXXIV

"You've been a pain in my ass since your birth. I cannot believe you talked me into rebelling against my king," Malcom muttered to Eddison.

Malcom had been watching over Eddison all his life. It was highly frowned upon for a guardian to get involved in their assigned's life, but Malcom failed Eddison repeatedly and needed to show that he was still capable of protecting him.

"She has been through unspeakable horrors; no amount of time can correct that. We can keep her comfortable for the rest of her days," Malcom stated, watching Kelby carefully pick up his mother and bring her towards a place where she could rest.

"I never believed in fate or its ability to control me, but I am the gatekeeper of the Heavens, meant to mate with its king," Eddison muttered and looked towards Dinah, who was talking to Everard in the distance.

Malcom thought about what he was going to say. "Dinah planned this liberation of Heaven and overthrew its corrupt ruler. It only seems fitting she would be selected to guard it."

The moment Mora fell unconscious a warmth overtook Dinah. The pain in breathing the air was no more, but she didn't know about her upgrade until Kace mentioned her golden feathers. She should have been upset, but instead, she got to work on learning what their next step would be.

"Like all kings, the world they command and its people are what give them the power. I thought you were supposed to be smart," Malcom teased.

Dinah groaned and glared at her now golden wings.

"What did you expect? You have been planning this since your release, and it was bound to happen," Everard mentioned.

"I don't want it," Dinah snapped.

"Well, you got it," Vadim replied, as it seemed he was late to the party.

Kelby. Hadwin. Everard. The three of them gathered around Dinah and waited for her to tell them what to do. They were all loyal, but once they heard Reid was detained by the king, they wanted to know why. For Vadim and Qued, Reid's capture eased any doubt they had if they made the correct decision in rebelling.

"Are you positive Reid is in Hell?" Dinah asked Vadim.

"Yes, and Nobu will know we all betrayed him if we go in after Reid. There is no element of surprise," Vadim explained.

Their voices were heard. They no longer needed to use their hands to communicate, but on the battlefield, not making any sound came in handy. It would be a skill they'd never lose.

"Which means we have only one shot," Hadwin added and glanced over to Navar and Kace.

"This was too easy . . .," Navar muttered, expecting something bad to happen.

"It was strategic, not easy. Many lives were lost in Mora's bloodlust that gave us this opening," Kace informed.

The only one who wasn't gathered in the great hall was Nova. She was wandering around the castle aimlessly. Her mind was elsewhere when she walked right into a woman who steadied her from falling.

The woman had a gentle face, but the uniform she wore was that of the Reapers. Death. Black leather with white symbols of the god of death. The Reapers guide the undead to a life beyond their physical body. If one was here, that means someone was going to be taken.

"Relax, Nova, I am not here for anyone," she said softly.

Nova's eyes then registered the red hair. It was as red as hers. Navar saw the encounter and tried to run to Nova, but he was blocked by an invisible force.

"I am not here to cause any alarm; I need to speak to your father," she said, not letting Nova go.

"Why is a Reaper here?" Willow whispered and all kings looked out the window.

"She looks like him . . .," Raynar growled, referring to a man he knew well.

Eddison walked out towards the garden and to his daughter's side. Everyone was quiet, waiting to see what was said, but the conversation only lasted a few moments, then Nova was in Navar's arms, and Eddison walked up to Raynar.

"What is wrong?" Dinah demanded to know.

"Can you gain me access to the Vampire Realm?" Eddison asked the Demon king.

"You won't be safe—"

"I am not concerned about my safety, I need entrance."

Raynar crossed his arms. "By crossing into Hell as the gatekeeper of Heaven, you are putting not only your life but your wife's life in the balance."

"If you want me to get Selene back, I need to go," Eddison explained.

Raynar only nodded. Before he joined the rebellion, the king was bloodthirsty and ruthless, but now that he had a family of his own, he learned the value of protecting the ones you loved. If this was a way to get Selene back, he would take it, regardless of the headache it would cause.

XXXV

"Selene, look, I made this for you," Faith said, showing her the picture she drew.

It was of all the redheads that currently sat around the dinner table. Selene didn't know how to read or speak the Vampire language, but she understood what the child did. She was a prisoner here, and even though Faith was trying to be nice, Selene wanted to leave.

"Did Father cause that shiner on her face?" Katarina whispered to William.

William and Katarina shared the same face. The Reapers now had their hoods down and they too shared each other's faces, but they knew Selene was at their mercy, regardless of whether they were gatekeepers to their promised worlds.

"It seems we have been invaded . . .," William muttered when a guard came into the room and handed William a parchment.

The way he said it was calm. An invasion could mean anything, but Selene was the one to jump up and run out the door as quickly as possible. She expected someone to follow but no one did. Faith was disappointed, but her father told her to stay seated because they were expecting a few more visitors.

Selene opened the large doors to get outside but was tripped, and fell into a pool of darkness. The energy that fueled the lights came from the stars, and if that force was interrupted, the world would be swallowed. But Selene needed to see the sun, to feel the sun on her skin, and the happiness Hell refused to give her.

"I can smell your fear," a male voice whispered.

"I want to go home," Selene begged, tears falling down her face.

"You lost control, Selene. You always had your father until he died, and then you had Reid. When he was taken away from you, and the children couldn't find you, the feeling of loneliness overtook you."

Selene lost all motivation to fight. All the need to breathe, to move, ceased, and she lay there, waiting for death to follow. She wanted the darkness to swallow her whole and take away this pain.

"This is what I feared," a female voice said.

"Even though Selene is Hell's gatekeeper, she never experienced its darkness. It was wrong of Reid to keep her away; she isn't strong enough to face him," the male voice added.

Those voices consumed her, causing Selene to curl up into a ball and scream. She lived in the Mortal world her entire life, and this darkness, this evil that touched her, hurt. The pain needed to stop.

"Follow my voice . . .," Eddison whispered into the darkness.

"No . . .," Selene cried.

"There is nothing to fear. The darkness is a part of you. Breathe, Selene, you are not alone anymore."

Selene reached out towards the voice and felt her brother's hand. Eddison pulled her close and a wave of power was sent towards them. Selene braced for impact, but a wave of feathers surrounded her, protecting her. Kace. Nova. Arc. Ash. Malla. Tallia. The six circled them, preventing anyone from coming close.

The darkness was absorbed and the lights from the outside illuminated the area. Two figures circled them, both with the same face. Red hair. Dark eyes. They were not a child of a gatekeeper; these two had a stronger power.

One wore the robes of the Reapers and the other of Seers. Two neutral forces that held the balance in check. Those individuals continued to circle, and Arc was the first one to finally break the silence.

"Why are you attacking my mother?" he demanded.

"She is weak," the man wearing the Seer robes responded.

"If you are going to save your father, she needs to become one with this world. The world she was meant to protect," the female added.

When they stopped, a familiar sound to Selene was heard. Two small boys crawled out from behind the two gatekeepers, crawling towards their mother. Her babies. Selene continued to cry as she reached for her sons, and when she got them in her arms, everything around her ceased to exist.

XXXVI

They all gathered inside once the tension eased. The children of Selene and Eddison filled one side, and the relations of the other set of twins were on the other. A brother and a sister. Selene never knew more of her blood existed, but she was focused on her children, not the people that were talking about her.

"Look how he stands, I swear that man is the rising eighth general," Aberdeen, brother to Ibitzee, said as they both watched Kace pace around the room.

With the influx of gatekeepers, they could not stay in Hell. The fear of Nobu knowing about this many gatekeepers took precedent over controlling the portals. The only safe place was the neutral territories, and it was the Seer castle they found themselves in.

"Why would a general train a gatekeeper?" Ibitzee asked her brother as that side of the room continued to watch Kace.

The realm of the Seer was protected and secure. Not even Nobu could enter, which made this the safest place they all could be.

"The Dragons, Fae, Siren, Demon, Spirit, and Elf are all connected. We do not even know what those two infants

S. G. Blinn

will control in the future. One family holds a lot of power in their grasp," Katarina muttered to her brother, William.

There was a clear separation between the families. Nova was getting tired of all this waiting. She drew a sword from underneath her belt and walked towards Selene.

"Do not remove her chain!" Eddison said, knowing what his daughter intended.

"Father—"

"It is preventing Nobu from sensing her. Even in the neutral realm, the king can sense their gatekeeper," Kace explained.

Kace was tired of waiting too. Against what his father stated, he walked out of the room, ignoring the screams to come back. The only magic blocked was Selene's, and when Kace walked outside, he looked at the generals in front of him.

The sanction was for gatekeepers only; the generals were forbidden to enter. They all were ready for battle, wearing their armor with the markings of the King of Hell removed. Kace went up to his mother, the only one amongst them with golden wings, and frowned.

"You can't be here," he stated.

"We are the only ones who know the castle. If indeed Reid is with Nobu, your mother is the only one who can prepare Selene on what to expect when Nobu finds her," Kelby stated.

Kace didn't take his eyes off his mother. "Did you know Selene and Father had a brother and a sister?"

242

"Come with me," Dinah said and walked away from the group.

Dinah walked around the front of the castle and towards the side, away from prying eyes. Golden wings were always a symbol of the Heavenly king, but when Dinah approached a woman with black wings on her back, there was a different feeling coming from her.

That woman's hair was not red, but she had the wings the generals passed to their children. Along with the wings, her hair was white, and her jeweled eyes were dark. Her robes indicated she was royalty, and with this being the Seer realm, Kace knew he was looking at the Seer king.

"You're half Human" was Dinah's first statement.

"What do you want to prove with the six of you being here today?" she asked.

"The Hellion in all of us can sense our own king. I and Reid are the only ones with children. My brothers have sired no young, yet here you are, a second generation. Who made you?" Dinah asked.

She didn't answer at first but thought about what to say to Dinah to avoid a conflict.

"Selene is not ready to face Nobu. Her children will distract her. This war needs to end, and it needs Selene to seal its fate."

Dinah took a step forward. "You birthed some of the gatekeepers in the castle. Blood is strong and can tell a story. Those with dark wings are of your blood, yet they hold the blood related to my husband. How is this possible?"

Katarina was the gatekeeper to the Shifters, and her brother, William, was the gatekeeper to the Vampires. They were both of royal blood, the Seer's blood, but the Reapers, they shared no wings and were not one of hers. Four. There were four gatekeepers in existence who had the power to repopulate a lost world. Two more than anyone ever thought could exist.

"You figure it out," the Seer king observed.

"If you want Selene, she comes with her family. Will that be a problem?" Dinah asked.

"My father was right about you . . .," she muttered.

"And what was that?"

The Seer king smirked. "You are the only general born with the ability to feel love or emotion without training. It is not because you are a woman. Mora held you in her arms and gave you that gift to plan her escape. You were born with a curse, and you broke that curse when you gained a higher purpose."

Dinah scoffed. "You're the King of the Seers, you foresaw this exact moment and know what is to come but you will not tell me . . ."

Dinah was done talking. She would rescue Reid with or without the help of the others. Those who didn't choose a side forfeit the right to fight. With the six generals together against the man who created them, the curse would not only be lifted from Dinah but from all those who were stained by the blood of war.

XXXVII

"Are you certain Mora has been defeated?" Nobu asked no one in particular.

It couldn't be true. The images he was seeing before him were a lie.

"All Angelic forces have been withdrawn, and word is spreading of a mysterious woman who defeated her," a minion reported.

"My council?"

The creature bowed in front of his angry king. "Summoned as requested."

Nobu was always in control. Power. Strength. Fear. It was the pillar of how he controlled everything in his life. Without his generals, he will lose everything he had built. They no longer wore his mark, which meant Nobu could no longer see what was happening.

Less than one hundred kings sat in a circular room in his castle. They were waiting for the king they despised but knew better than to go up against.

"He lost all his generals. He lost more than half his strength," a king muttered.

"You're brooding," Wallixa, the Banshee king, muttered to the Vampire right next to her.

245

"I am going to destroy Raynar for allowing the rebellion to come into my home unannounced," the Vampire king muttered.

Everyone was talking about the loss of the generals and the mysterious woman who overthrew Heaven. When Nobu entered the room, no one stood, but they did fall silent to see what he had to say.

"My Kings—"

Nobu was only able to mutter a few words before everyone looked towards the closed door behind him. A radiating power was felt which caused the lights above to flicker. Nobu knew this power, and it no longer belonged to Mora.

Dinah stood in the middle of her father's throne room wearing the golden armor of the Heavens. She paced slowly around her father's throne but never sat. This chair was a symbol, one of power that he no longer had, and that brought her a small joy, knowing she was a part of his downfall.

"This room was always cold like the rest of the castle. There isn't an ounce of warmth, no matter how hard I look," Dinah said and looked up to the open door, right into her father's cold eyes.

Nobu did not hear a word his daughter spoke. His attention was to the golden wings. His blood ran through her veins, yet she carried the crown of the one place he could never touch. A kingdom that he could never conquer.

"I hope her death was painful," he muttered.

"My mother is an extremely sick woman. Years of abuse can destroy a mind. Break a spirit. You tried it with me and failed," Dinah replied.

"You were nothing more than a failure to a perfect experiment," Nobu replied.

Dinah's expression did not change: she refused to allow him any satisfaction.

"No, Father, you are the one who is nothing and fell right into my trap."

When Nobu went to take a step forward, he vanished. Eddison was sitting behind the throne, being the air his wife needed to breathe, and the comfort to convince her she will not be trapped within these walls again.

"The kings?" Dinah asked, looking to the glowing symbols on the ground where Nobu once stood.

"Contained," Eddison replied.

Dinah took a deep breath, trying to regain her composure. She faced him, the man who caused all her pain, but she feared the trap would not hold long enough for them to find Reid.

*

Five minutes. That was what the gatekeepers told the generals the trap would hold. For six months all the gatekeepers in existence used their power to plan this attack. The kings could not be involved, not officially, but they offered every resource. Will it be enough?

"This is bigger than we thought," Kace muttered, using his wings for speed to check every room in the hallway he was assigned.

"Stop complaining," Nova muttered, checking the other side of the hallway.

Endless hallways. A map was drawn by the ones who used to live there, but everyone only had minutes to cover it. They lacked bodies, it wasn't enough time, but they had to try.

"Nope," Katarina stated, closing a door quickly.

Empty spaces. Not a soul filled these rooms. Nothingness. They were running out of time.

*

"Don't give in," Selene whispered to herself, shaking in the middle of the banquet hall.

She had to stay out of sight, but Selene heard every pain, every scream Nobu had caused. When she entered the castle, she felt a pull she couldn't shake. It brought her to this room, and she was terrified.

"Stop . . .," she whined and closed her eyes.

Tick. Tock. Each passing minute, those voices grew louder, and a sudden crack in her surroundings caused Selene to open her eyes. Nobu. The chain on her leg slowly started to dissolve as the voices in her head grew louder.

"You are supposed to be dead," Nobu whispered.

"Don't touch me!" she snapped, trembling in the presence of the Hellion king.

248

A Witch. A gatekeeper. A crooked smile formed on his face as the final piece to his puzzle was delivered to him. His reign would never be threatened if he had his key, and he found her, right here in his home.

"Get away from me!" Selene screamed, covering her ears, trying to drown out the screams.

"How long have you been alive? To be able to avoid my detection means my general failed. He never fails me."

This was Hell. It took away all hopes, happiness, and light. Unless the individual was prepared, there was no way a non-Hellion could survive in its darkness. Eddison had Dinah to give him a protective shield, but without Reid and her children, Selene didn't have the strength to beat him.

Nobu reached forward and took a strand of her red hair between his fingers. He brought it to his nose and took in a deep breath.

"So beautiful. So perfect. You are mine—"

When Nobu leaned forward, a power pushed them both apart. Nobu hit the ground hard, and Selene looked towards a third person with a horrified expression on her face.

Poles. Chains. Straps. Reid's body was covered in bruises, holes, and lash marks. He was tortured for months, rendered unconscious by his father's power. He could not fight back until a stronger power broke into Nobu's castle, one that woke him up long enough to feel Selene in a place she should not be.

"This place can only be accessed if I allow it. Only She and I can be here, but you . . . you failed me!" Nobu yelled to Reid, whose blood slowly pooled underneath him.

Reid could barely stand, let alone breathe, but he was in between his father and lover, protecting her even when he could no longer fight.

"Reid . . ."

"You are the gatekeeper of Hell—" Nobu yelled, but Reid slowly and painfully turned to look at his wife.

"Remember our children, their laughter and smiles. Hold onto that, and the darkness will never touch you," he said painfully, blood dripping from his mouth.

"Of course, you mated with her! I want every one of your bastard children destroyed!" Nobu yelled, and Reid looked behind Selene, seeing the figure from the sky.

Nobu felt a calm in seeing the man, the one with Reid's face. That man moved with extreme speed and thrust a gold dagger into Reid's stomach. He kicked Selene away, but his speed—no one saw his actions until it was too late to react.

Selene went to scream, but when she blinked, she was back in the banquet hall and Reid was nowhere to be found. There was one other there with her, the one that shared Reid's face and had his blood dripping from his hands. Selene went to fight, to scream, but when that man picked her up, she fell into a deep sleep in his arms.

William burst open the door and looked at the man. There was no shock, no surprise in seeing him. He watched as the man put Selene in his arms and put the dagger back in his belt.

"I want the kings out of the castle," he said and took two steps away before he stopped.

Kelby. Hadwin. Everard. They all stood on one end, and when the man looked behind him, Dinah, Vadim, and Qued were at the other side. No blades were visible from the generals, but they were defensive towards a person they didn't know.

"There was always seven of us, never eight," Dinah said, and the man looked towards Katarina, who barreled through Kelby and Hadwin, not realizing what was happening.

"The castle has been evacuated . . .," she trailed off when she saw everyone in the hallway.

"Take all the gatekeepers back to your mother. Wait for me to send word it is safe to return," the man said.

He was the father of the King of the Seers. William. Katarina. They held his blood. The man opened his wings and flapped them hard, vanishing at a speed that no one could trace. Ibitzee and her brother dragged an unconscious Reid out of the banquet hall, bloodied and on the brink of death.

Reid. His twin. Nobu. All their efforts were for this final moment, but in looking at Reid and Selene, rather than feel the rejoice in Nobu's power no longer being felt, the unease about this new man created a new level of fear. Nobu. He was trapped in a place no one could access, his body torn apart and lifeless. The one man he trusted, allowed to call him father, was the one man that had to do the deed, to free his siblings from the chain around their neck since the moment they were born.

Epilogue

Eight Years Later

Reid's existence was planned by two enemies to gain power. His constant battle with himself and his duty to the King of Hell created an unpredictable power when he found love with Selene. That love is what saved him but doomed him to a path of pain.

"Daddy?" a small boy whispered.

Reid's body went from a cold, empty feeling, to warm and numb. Smell. A need to see who spoke that word to him took the pain and violence he was in, out of his mind. Touch. A feeling of comfort from an unfamiliar weight on his arm, one that almost felt welcoming.

"Please, daddy, wake up," another small voice said.

Everyone feared the firstborn general. He was hated for his allegiance to his father, one forced upon him with pain, violence, and fear. But when he opened his eyes, two redheaded boys looked down at him with tears in their eyes.

He could sense those boys were his. But his sons were both babies. Mica and Lee were children now, with tears falling down their faces. It hurt to move, but Reid wrapped his arms around them, holding them close.

"Welcome back," Eddison said gently.

Monitors and machines covered the room. Holding onto his boys, Reid realized he was in a hospital room, one in the Mortal world.

"Your guardians are here, boys. Your father will be here when you get back," Eddison whispered, and they both nodded.

Reid looked at his sons and saw they were wearing the garments of two races. Had they found their kings? No, he still had time with them before their duty took them away. The panic was in his face, but when his sons wiped their tears away and said goodbye, he realized he needed their strength to understand what happened.

"I want them back . . .," Reid whispered, trying to get his emotions under control.

"Mica and Lee are on a rotating schedule between Heaven, Hell, and their kings' realms. A schedule we cannot interrupt while you heal."

"My boys . . ."

"You are safe, Reid. Your family, all of them are safe. Let me get you checked out before we have a talk," Eddison said and slowly administered a sedative to calm him down so he can finally assess a man who had been asleep for over eight years.

*

He lost so much time. When Reid woke up, Eddison explained his wings were damaged beyond repair. They were wrapped tightly to his body to avoid them from decaying.

"My body should be healed if I had eight years to heal . . .," Reid muttered, slowly pacing in Eddison's office the next day.

"Considering your wounds were made by a holy weapon forged from the king's soul, I am surprised it didn't take longer."

"Where am I?" Reid asked, looking to Eddison sitting behind his desk.

"The Mortal world; and I need you to listen to me. A lot has happened because of Nobu's death. There is no body, but the Reapers confirmed that he has passed, and his body destroyed. I need—"

"Selene!" Reid yelled when a vision of his wife scared in the castle crossed his mind.

He couldn't remember everything. The memories were slowly coming back—but Selene, what happened to her, what happened to his wife? Before Eddison could respond, Reid was out of the door and surprisingly, no one stopped him.

This hospital was located near the mountains of the moon clan. The smell in the air . . . he knew that smell. This was his home, his sanctuary, and when Reid burst through the doors, it was quiet, too quiet.

"Selene!" he called out, painfully moving quickly from room to room.

He might not have his wings, but he had his abilities granted by his royal parents. He could move fast, get to where he needed to go. When he opened the door to the kitchen, a man stood there. His back was to him, but the black wings and slim body shape told Reid exactly who it was.

"Before you attack me, Reid, I want you to realize I had to do what was necessary, not only to protect my family but yours as well," he spoke.

"Face me, you coward!"

His face was Reid's face. The only difference between the two men was their body types. Reid was built for combat, a warrior, but this man, he was built for stealth and speed. A man who was his twin brother.

"Our father never told you, nor anyone, of my existence as a failsafe. Not even our mother knew I existed, the perfect assassin. He called me Zero, a number, but in his mind a name, one worthy of a son whom he could trust—"

"Why?" Reid demanded.

"Our mother gave all her children a name, one she whispered the moment they were born. And like you, I found solace in a single individual I grew to love and wanted to protect. IT didn't matter who got her, I needed—"

Reid took two giant steps towards Zero, but his twin held up a golden feather. Reid stopped dead in his tracks and looked at the feather. It wasn't Dinah's, he would have felt its power. Footsteps crept up behind him, but Reid didn't react.

"I know I am running late, but Reid is having a harder time processing everything than I thought. Go tell the others I will be there shortly," he said to the figure behind Reid and those footsteps walked away.

"I—"

Zero wouldn't let Reid speak.

"I met my wife, a Human woman, when I was only twenty-seven years old. You and the other generals were still training when I was killing those whom Nobu thought as his enemy. That woman challenged me, made me think in ways I never thought possible, and when our child came into the world, she gave me a gift I never knew I needed."

"The Seer king?" Reid asked, remembering the whispers of the conversations around him when he was healing in the hospital.

"How my daughter became the king isn't a story you need to hear, but I loved my wife. I held her when she died of old age and swore to her I'd protect our child, the only thing I had left of her. I have a family that is bound to yours by blood, not from me, but from the gatekeepers who grow in population. This will not be the last time you see me, but this will be the last time I have pity on you."

Reid turned and slowly walked out of the room. His head was spinning, but when he saw the Reaper King Eilee and Zero's daughter Everlynn, he paused. There was a woman and a man, twins with red hair and the same face next to them. Gatekeepers, their gatekeepers, who seemed to be comfortable in his home.

"I told you he wasn't dead," Eilee said, and Everlynn smirked.

"That you did."

"Dinah had formed an alliance with the neutral territories. Gatekeepers come in pairs, and her husband and your wife had a pair of older siblings they did not know about until recently. You failed to kill four gatekeepers, which in the end united the rebellion together," Zero said from behind Reid, who held the feather in his hand tightly.

"What do you want from me?" Reid asked.

"Your family can no longer live in this coven house. You need to make a choice if you are going to join them or not—"

"Where is my wife?" Reid yelled.

"We all work in the shadows to make sure the world stays balanced. Your rebellion is an example of how a world can unite under a common cause, but the gatekeepers are the ones that helped this world move forward."

Hadwin. Kelby. Vadim. Qued. Everard. They all looked down to Reid from the balcony above. They held no affiliations of Hell or any king; they were, in Reid's eyes, free.

"Selene is in Hell. With the help of your children and their spouses, they have been picking up the pieces our father shattered and helped the world heal. Rebuild a lost trust," Zero explained.

"Z," Vadim called out, and Reid looked away from his brothers.

"You know that feather is yours, Reid, not mine," Dinah began, walking into the room.

"I don't want this," Reid pleaded with her.

"The King of Heaven and Hell are not born; they are selected for their power. By dethroning Mora, I took her place. Because you fought Nobu, defying his orders to protect others and starting the rebellion, Hell chose you."

It took Reid only a moment from learning where Selene was to vanish. He heard about the choice, about what was expected of him, but he didn't care: he needed to see Selene. IF he was going to be the King of Hell, so be it, if he had his wife by his side.

*

Reid appeared on an outer wall of the Hellion castle and pulled his hood up to his jacket. This place was never one he would go to intentionally, but something felt different about it.

The stars above shined brightly, showing the power of Hell and the loyalty of its followers. Guards were posted at every column, every window, and their faces showed content over pain. Servants were talking about their day, no longer afraid to speak, and laughter filled the halls, a sound never heard in that space.

"Cameron, wait up!" Keva yelled and ran by Reid, who was hiding in the shadows.

The Fae and Dragon princes both held their royal markings, yet played in a place that should be forbidden. He so was lost in watching the children play that he didn't hear Raynar approach him from behind.

"You have questions," he observed.

"It is peaceful."

258

"You created a system that works in your absence. When news spread of Nobu's demise and your ascension, the Hellion races were too scared to rebel. Selene used her connections to the generals and their influence to help them and her overcome their fears, and rebuild what Nobu destroyed. The council will convene tomorrow; take the time you need to learn what has happened and talk to your wife. She is in the throne room."

Reid moved before Raynar could finish his sentence. Selene. He heard her sweet voice through the golden doors, and when she opened it, she walked right into his embrace.

Her red hair was pulled back tightly, and a black suit covered her body. The guards should have attacked him, but when Reid spread his golden wings, he wrapped them around her, protecting her from the world outside.

"You're here . . .," she whispered, knowing who held her tightly.

Reid's heart was racing, but all he could do was hold her. She was here, alive, and unharmed. He failed her and his children. Reid could not protect them and that thought made him hold onto her even tighter.

"You and I will be together. Never apart. I love you, Selene, and thank the gods you are in my life. I promise to always protect you. No more secrets, no more pain . . ."

While Reid reunited with his family, the rest of the generals traveled to many realms in many parts of the worlds to find themselves again. Nobu was gone, the war was over, but they still felt empty. They had no purpose, no direction, and with the world still remembering what they did, they needed to hide—except for Vadim.

He found solace in knowing his ward, Kace, requested him to be at his side, but Fae was a changing world. Heaven. Hell. They had their kings, their own problems, but this realm was about to face a challenge that no one expected, and if Vadim couldn't solve it, the peace they fought for could be taken away

The End

Read Vadim's Story

"Hellfire"

Seven Generals Book Two

Summer 2022

S. G. Blinn is an award-winning author that has been writing since she was in grade school. With an education in Media Arts and Digital Design, she brought to life a world that was trapped in her imagination. She designed the book cover for *A Drink With Death* that won the **AWAOA Best Book Cover Award 2022**. She also won the **AWAOA Spirit Award 2022**. Her debut novel *The Monster's Daughter* was released on 10/05/2021. Her first series novel *A Drink With Death: Where's Death Series* Book One was released on 01/25/2022.

Want to stay connected?
www.sgblinn.com